Gabriel García Márquez

Leaf Storm
and other stories

translated from the Spanish
by Gregory Rabassa

published by Pan Books

Leaf Storm was originally published in Spanish under the title
La Hojarasca

'The Handsomest Drowned Man in the World' originally appeared in
Playboy Magazine

'A Very Old Man with Enormous Wings' originally appeared in
New American Review

'Blacamán the Good, Vendor of Miracles' was first published in
Esquire Magazine

Grateful acknowledgement is given to the University of Chicago Press for
Sophocles' *Antigone*, translated by Elizabeth Wyckoff which appears in
Sophocles 1, edited by David Greene and Richmond Lattimore. Copyright
1954 by The University of Chicago. Reprinted by permission.

First published in Great Britain 1972 by Jonathan Cape Ltd,
This edition published 1979 by Pan Books Ltd,
Cavaye Place, London SW10 9PG
19 18 17 16 15 14 13 12
English translation © 1972 by Harper and Row, Publishers, Inc, New York
ISBN 0 330 25688 2
Printed and bound in Great Britain by
Cox & Wyman Ltd, Reading

But Polyneices' corpse who died in pain
they say he has proclaimed to the whole town
that none may bury him and none bewail,
but leave him unwept, untombed, a rich sweet sight
for the hungry birds' beholding.
Such orders they say the worthy Creon gives
to you and me—yes, yes, I say to me—
and that he's coming to proclaim it clear
to those who know it not.
Further: he has the matter so at heart
that anyone who dares attempt the act
will die by public stoning in the town.
Antigone

Contents

Leaf Storm

—Suddenly, as if a whirlwind had set down roots in the center of the town, the banana company arrived, pursued by the leaf storm. A whirling leaf storm had been stirred up, formed out of the human and material dregs of other towns, the chaff of a civil war that seemed ever more remote and unlikely. The whirlwind was implacable. It contaminated everything with its swirling crowd smell, the smell of skin secretion and hidden death. In less than a year it sowed over the town the rubble of many catastrophes that had come before it, scattering its mixed cargo of rubbish in the streets. And all of a sudden that rubbish, in time to the mad and unpredicted rhythm of the storm, was being sorted out, individualized, until what had been a narrow street with a river at one end and a corral for the dead at the other was changed into a different and more complex town, created out of the rubbish of other towns.

Arriving there, mingled with the human leaf storm, dragged along by its impetuous force, came the dregs of warehouses, hospitals, amusement parlors, electric plants; the dregs made up of single women and men who tied their mules to hitching posts by the hotel, carrying their single piece of baggage, a wooden trunk or a bundle of clothing, and in a few months each had his own house, two mistresses, and the military title that was due him for having arrived late for the war.

Even the dregs of the cities' sad love came to us in the whirlwind and built small wooden houses where at first a corner and a half-cot were a dismal home for one night, and then a noisy clandestine street, and then a whole inner village of tolerance within the town.

In the midst of that blizzard, that tempest of unknown faces, of awnings along the public way, of men changing clothes in the street, of women with open parasols sitting on trunks, and of mule after abandoned mule dying of hunger on the block by the hotel, the first of us came to be the last; we were the outsiders, the newcomers.

After the war, when we came to Macondo and appreciated the good quality of its soil, we knew that the leaf storm was sure to come someday, but we did not count on its drive. So when we felt the avalanche arrive, the only thing we could do was set a plate with a knife and fork behind the door and sit patiently waiting for the newcomers to get to know us. Then the train whistled for the first time. The leaf storm turned about and went out to greet it, and by turning it lost its drive. But it developed unity and mass; and it underwent the natural process of fermentation, becoming incorporated into the germination of the earth.

Macondo, 1909

I.

I've seen a corpse for the first time. It's Wednesday but I feel as if it was Sunday because I didn't go to school and they dressed me up in a green corduroy suit that's tight in some places. Holding Mama's hand, following my grandfather, who feels his way along with a cane with every step he takes so he won't bump into things (he doesn't see well in the dark and he limps), I went past the mirror in the living room and saw myself full length, dressed in green and with this white starched collar that pinches me on one side of the neck. I saw myself in the round mottled looking-glass and I thought: *That's me, as if today was Sunday.*

We've come to the house where the dead man is.

The heat won't let you breathe in the closed room. You can hear the sun buzzing in the streets, but that's all. The air is stagnant, like concrete; you get the feeling that it could get all twisted like a sheet of steel. In the room where they've laid out the corpse there's a smell of trunks, but I can't see any anywhere. There's a hammock in the corner hanging by one end from a ring. There's a smell of trash. And I think that the things around us, broken down and almost falling apart, have the look of things that ought to smell like trash even though they smell like something else.

I always thought that dead people should have hats on. Now I can see that they shouldn't. I can see that they have a head like wax and a handkerchief tied around their jawbone. I can see

3

that they have their mouth open a little and that behind the purple lips you can see the stained and irregular teeth. I can see that they keep their tongue bitten over to one side, thick and sticky, a little darker than the color of their face, which is like the color of fingers clutching a stick. I can see that they have their eyes open much wider than a man's, anxious and wild, and that their skin seems to be made of tight damp earth. I thought that a dead man would look like somebody quiet and asleep and now I can see that it's just the opposite. I can see that he looks like someone awake and in a rage after a fight.

Mama is dressed up as if it was Sunday too. She put on the old straw hat that comes down over her ears and a black dress closed at the neck and with sleeves that come down to her wrists. Since today is Wednesday she looks to me like someone far away, a stranger, and I get the feeling that she wants to tell me something when my grandfather gets up to receive the men who've brought the coffin. Mama is sitting beside me with her back to the closed door. She's breathing heavily and she keeps pushing back the strands of hair that fall out from under the hat that she put on in a hurry. My grandfather has told the men to put the coffin down next to the bed. Only then did I realize that the dead man could really fit into it. When the men brought in the box I had the impression that it was too small for a body that took up the whole length of the bed.

I don't know why they brought me along. I've never been in this house before and I even thought that nobody lived here. It's a big house, on the corner, and I don't think the door has ever been opened. I always thought that nobody lived in the house. Only now, after my mother told me, "You won't be going to school this afternoon," and I didn't feel glad because she said it with a serious and reserved voice, and I saw her come back with my corduroy suit and she put it on me without saying a word and we went to the door to join my grandfather, and we walked past the three houses that separated this one from ours, only now do I realize that someone lived on the corner. Someone who died and who must be the man my mother was talking about when she said: "You have to behave yourself at the doctor's funeral."

When we went in I didn't see the dead man. I saw my grandfather at the door talking to the men, and then I saw him telling us to go on in. I thought then that there was somebody in the room, but when I went in I felt it was dark and empty. The heat beat on my face from the very first minute and I got that trash smell that was solid and permanent at first and now, like the heat, comes in slow-spaced waves and disappears. Mama led me through the dark room by the hand and seated me next to her in a corner. Only after a moment could I begin to make things out. I saw my grandfather trying to open a window that seemed stuck to its frame, glued to the wood around it, and I saw him hitting his cane against the latches, his coat covered with the dust that came off with every blow. I turned my head to where my grandfather was moving as he said he couldn't open the window and only then did I see there was someone on the bed. There was a dark man stretched out, motionless. Then I spun my head to my mother's side where she sat serious and without moving, looking off somewhere else in the room. Since my feet don't touch the floor and hang in the air half a foot away, I put my hands under my thighs, placing the palms on the chair, and I began to swing my legs, not thinking about anything until I remembered that Mama had told me: "You have to behave yourself at the doctor's funeral." Then I felt something cold behind me. I turned to look and I only saw the wall of dry and pitted wood. But it was as if someone had said to me from the wall: *Don't move your legs. The man on the bed is the doctor and he's dead.* And when I looked toward the bed I didn't see him the way I had before. I didn't see him lying down, I saw him dead.

From then on, as much as I try not to look, I feel as if someone is forcing my face in that direction. And even if I make an effort to look at other places in the room, I see him just the same, everywhere, with his bulging eyes and his green, dead face in the shadows.

I don't know why no one has come to the wake. The ones who came are us, my grandfather, Mama, and the four Guajiro Indians who work for my grandfather. The men brought a sack of lime and emptied it inside the coffin. If my mother hadn't been strange and far away I would have asked her why they did it. I don't understand why they have to sprinkle lime inside the box. When the bag was empty one of the men shook it over the coffin and a few last flakes fell out, looking more like sawdust than lime. They lifted the dead man by the shoulders and feet. He's wearing a pair of cheap pants tied at the waist by a wide black cord, and a gray shirt. He only has his left shoe on. As Ada says, he's got one foot a king and the other one a slave. The right shoe is at one end of the bed. On the bed the dead man seemed to be having trouble. In the coffin he looks more comfortable, more peaceful, and his face, which had been like the face of a man who was alive and awake after a fight, has taken on a restful and secure look. His profile is softer. It's as if in the box there he now felt he was in his proper place as a dead man.

My grandfather's been moving around the room. He's picked up some things and put them in the box. I look at Mama again hoping that she'll tell me why my grandfather is tossing things into the coffin. But my mother is unmoved in her black dress and she seems to be making an effort not to look where the dead man is. I try to do the same thing but I can't. I stare at him. I examine him. My grandfather throws a book inside the coffin, signals the men, and three of them put the lid over the corpse. Only then do I feel free of the hands that were holding my head toward that side and I begin to look the room over.

I look at my mother again. For the first time since we came to the house she looks at me and smiles with a forced smile, with nothing inside; and in the distance I can hear the train whistle as

6

it disappears around the last bend. I hear a sound from the corner where the corpse is. I see one of the men lift one edge of the lid and my grandfather puts the dead man's shoe into the coffin, the shoe they had forgotten on the bed. The train whistles again, farther off, and suddenly I think: *It's two-thirty.* I remember that it's the time (when the train whistles at the last bend in town) when the boys line up at school to go in for the first class in the afternoon.

Abraham, I think.

I shouldn't have brought the child. A spectacle like this isn't proper for him. Even for myself, turning thirty, this atmosphere thinned out by the presence of the corpse is harmful. We could leave now. We could tell Papa that we don't feel well in a room where the remains of a man cut off from everything that could be considered affection or thanks have been accumulating for seventeen years. My father may be the only one who's ever shown any feeling for him. An inexplicable feeling that's been of use to him now so he won't rot away inside these four walls.

I'm bothered by how ridiculous all of this is. I'm upset by the idea that in a moment we'll be going out into the street following a coffin that won't inspire any feeling except pleasure in anyone. I can imagine the expression on the faces of the women in the windows, watching my father go by, watching me go by with the child behind a casket inside of which the only person the town has wanted to see that way is rotting away, on his way to the cemetery in the midst of unyielding abandonment, followed by three people who decided to perform a work of charity that's been the beginning of his own vengeance. It could be that this decision of Papa's could mean that tomorrow there won't be anyone prepared to walk behind our funeral processions.

Maybe that's why I brought the child along. When Papa told me a moment ago: "You have to go with me," the first thing that occurred to me was to bring the child so that I would feel

7

protected. Now here we are on this suffocating September afternoon, feeling that the things around us are the pitiless agents of our enemies. Papa's got no reason to worry. Actually, he's spent his whole life doing things like this; giving the town stones to chew on, keeping his most insignificant promises with his back turned to all convention. Since that time twenty-five years ago when this man came to our house, Papa must have imagined (when he noticed the visitor's absurd manners) that today there wouldn't be a single person in the whole town prepared even to throw his body to the buzzards. Maybe Papa foresaw all the obstacles and measured and calculated the possible inconveniences. And now, twenty-five years later, he must feel that this is just the fulfillment of a chore he's thought about for a long time, one which had to be carried out in any case, since he would have had to haul the corpse through the streets of Macondo by himself.

Still, when the time came, he didn't have the courage to do it alone and he made me take part in that intolerable promise that he must have made long before I even had the use of reason. When he told me: "You have to go with me," he didn't give me time to think about how far his words went; I couldn't calculate how much shame and ridicule there would be in burying this man whom everyone had hoped to see turn to dust inside his lair. Because people hadn't just expected that, they'd prepared themselves for things to happen that way and they'd hoped for it from the bottom of their hearts, without remorse, and even with the anticipated satisfaction of someday smelling the pleasant odor of his decomposition floating through the town without anyone's feeling moved, alarmed, or scandalized, satisfied rather at seeing the longed-for hour come, wanting the situation to go on and on until the twirling smell of the dead man would satisfy even the most hidden resentments.

Now we're going to deprive Macondo of its long-desired pleasure. I feel as if in a certain way this determination of ours has

8

given birth in the hearts of the people not to a melancholy feeling of frustration but to one of postponement.

That's another reason why I should have left the child at home; so as not to get him mixed up in this conspiracy which will center on us now the way it did on the doctor for ten years. The child should have been left on the sidelines of this promise. He doesn't even know why he's here, why we've brought him to this room full of rubbish. He doesn't say anything, sitting, swinging his legs with his hands resting on the chair, waiting for someone to decipher this frightful riddle for him. I want to be sure that nobody will, that no one will open that invisible door that prevents him from going beyond the reach of his senses.

He's looked at me several times and I know that he finds me strange, somebody he doesn't know, with this stiff dress and this old hat that I've put on so that I won't be identified even by my own forebodings.

If Meme were alive, here in the house, maybe it would have been different. They might have thought I came because of her. They might have thought I came to share in a grief that she probably wouldn't have felt, but which she would have been able to pretend and which the town could have explained. Meme disappeared about eleven years ago. The doctor's death has ended any possibility of finding out where she is or, at least, where her bones are. Meme isn't here, but it's most likely that if she were— if what happened and was never cleared up hadn't happened—she would have taken the side of the town against the man who warmed her bed for six years with as much love and humanity as a mule might have had.

I can hear the train whistling at the last bend. *It's two-thirty*, I think; and I can't get rid of the idea that at this moment all of Macondo is wondering what we're doing in this house. I think about Señora Rebeca, thin and looking like parchment, with the touch of a family ghost in her look and dress, sitting beside her

9

electric fan, her face shaded by the screens in her windows. As she hears the train disappearing around the last bend Señora Rebeca leans her head toward the fan, tormented by the heat and her resentment, the blades in her heart spinning like those on the fan (but in an opposite direction), and she murmurs: "The devil has a hand in all of this," and she shudders, fastened to life by the tiny roots of everyday things.

And Águeda, the cripple, seeing Solita coming back from the station after seeing her boyfriend off; seeing her open her parasol as she turns the deserted corner; hearing her approach with the sexual rejoicing that she herself once had and which changed inside her into that patient religious sickness that makes her say: "You'll wallow in your bed like a pig in its sty."

I can't get rid of that idea. Stop thinking that it's two-thirty; that the mule with the mail is going by cloaked in a burning cloud of dust and followed by the men who have interrupted their Wednesday siesta to pick up the bundles of newspapers. Father Ángel is dozing, sitting in the sacristy with an open breviary on his greasy stomach, listening to the mule pass and shooting away the flies that are bothering his sleep, belching, saying: "You poisoned me with your meatballs."

Papa's cold-blooded about all this. Even to the point of telling them to open the coffin so they could put in the shoe that was left on the bed. Only he could have taken an interest in that man's meanness. I wouldn't be surprised if when we leave with the corpse the crowd will be waiting for us with all the excrement they could get together overnight and will give us a shower of filth for going against the will of the town. Maybe they won't do it because of Papa. Maybe they will do it because it's something as terrible as frustrating a pleasure the town had longed for over so many years, thought about on stifling afternoons whenever men and women passed this house and said to themselves: "Sooner or later we'll lunch on that smell." Because that's what they all said, from the first to the last.

It'll be three o'clock in a little while. The Señorita already knows it. Señora Rebeca saw her pass and called her, invisible behind the screen, and she came out from the orbit of the fan for a moment and said to her: "Señorita, it's the devil, you know." And tomorrow it won't be my son who goes to school but some other, completely different child; a child who will grow, reproduce, and die in the end with no one paying him the debt of gratitude which would give him Christian burial.

I'd probably be peacefully at home right now if twenty-five years ago that man hadn't come to my father's home with a letter of recommendation (no one ever knew where he came from), if he hadn't stayed with us, eating grass and looking at women with those eyes of a lustful dog that popped out of their sockets. But my punishment was written down from before my birth and it stayed hidden, repressed, until that fateful leap year when I would turn thirty and my father would tell me: "You have to go with me." And then, before I had time to ask anything, he pounded the floor with his cane: "We have to go through with this just the way it is, daughter. The doctor hanged himself this morning."

The men left and came back to the room with a hammer and a box of nails. But they hadn't nailed up the coffin. They laid the things on the table and they sat on the bed where the dead man had been. My grandfather seems calm, but his calmness is imperfect and desperate. It's not the calmness of the corpse in the coffin, it's the calmness of an impatient man making an effort not to show how he feels. It's a rebellious and anxious calm, the kind my grandfather has, walking back and forth across the room, limping, picking up the clustered objects.

When I discover that there are flies in the room I begin to be tortured by the idea that the coffin's become full of flies. They still haven't nailed it shut, but it seems to me that the buzzing I thought at first was an electric fan in the neighborhood is the swarm of flies beating blindly against the sides of the coffin and the face of the dead man. I shake my head; I close my eyes; I see my grandfather open a trunk and take out some things and I can't tell what they are; on the bed I can see the four embers but not the people with the lighted cigars. Trapped by the suffocating heat, by the minute that doesn't pass, by the buzzing of the flies, I feel as if someone is telling me: *That's the way you'll be. You'll be inside a coffin filled with flies. You're only a little under eleven years old, but someday you'll be like that, left to the flies inside of a closed box.* And I stretch my legs out side by side and look at my own black and shiny boots. *One of my laces is untied,* I think and I look at Mama again. She looks at me too and leans over to tie my shoelace.

The vapor that rises up from Mama's head, warm and smelling like a cupboard, smelling of sleeping wood, reminds me of the closed-in coffin again. It becomes hard for me to breathe, I want to get out of here; I want to breathe in the burning street air, and I use my last resort. When Mama gets up I say to her in a low voice: "Mama!" She smiles, says: "Umm?" And I lean toward her, toward her raw and shining face, trembling. "I feel like going out back."

Mama calls my grandfather, tells him something. I watch his narrow, motionless eyes behind his glasses when he comes over and tells me: "That's impossible right now." I stretch and then remain quiet, indifferent to my failure. But things start to pass too slowly again. There's a rapid movement, another, and another. And then Mama leans over my shoulder again, saying: "Did it go away yet?" And she says it with a serious and solid voice, as if it was a scolding more than a question. My stomach is tight and hard, but Mama's question softens it, leaves it full and relaxed, and then everything, even her seriousness, becomes aggressive and challenging to me. "No," I tell her. "It still hasn't gone away." I squeeze in my stomach and try to beat the floor with my feet (another last resort), but I only find empty space below, the distance separating me from the floor.

Someone comes into the room. It's one of my grandfather's men, followed by a policeman and a man who is wearing green denim pants. He has a belt with a revolver on it and in his hand he's holding a hat with a broad, curled brim. My grandfather goes over to greet him. The man in the green pants coughs in the darkness, says something to my grandfather, coughs again; and still coughing he orders the policeman to open the window.

The wooden walls have a slippery look. They seem to be built of cold, compressed ash. When the policeman hits the latch with the butt of his rifle, I have the feeling that the shutters will not open. The house will fall down, the walls will crumble, but noiselessly, like a palace of ash collapsing in the wind. I feel that with a second blow we'll be in the street, in the sunlight, sitting down, our heads covered with debris. But with the second blow the shutter opens and light comes into the room; it bursts in violently, as when a gate is opened for a disoriented animal, who runs and smells, mute; who rages and scratches on the walls, slavering, and then goes back to flop down peacefully in the coolest corner of the cage.

With the window open things become visible, but consolidated in their strange unrealness. Then Mama takes a deep breath, takes me by the hand, and tells me: "Come, let's take a look at our house through the window." And I see the town again, as if I were returning to it after a trip. I can see our house, faded and run down, but cool under the almond trees; and I feel from here as if I'd never been inside that green and cordial coolness, as if ours were the perfect imaginary house promised by my mother on nights when I had bad dreams. And I see Pepe, who passes by without seeing us, lost in his thoughts. The boy from the house next door, who passes whistling, changed and unknown, as if he'd just had his hair cut off.

Then the mayor gets up, his shirt open, sweaty, his expression completely upset. He comes over to me all choked up by the excitement brought on by his own argument. "We can't be sure that he's dead until he starts to smell," he says, and he finishes buttoning up his shirt and lights a cigarette, his face turned toward the coffin again, thinking perhaps: *Now they can't say that I don't operate inside the law.* I look into his eyes and I feel that I've looked at him with enough firmness to make him understand that I can penetrate his deepest thoughts. I tell him: "You're operating outside the law in order to please the others." And he, as if that had been exactly what he had expected to hear, answers: "You're a respectable man, colonel. You know that I'm within my rights." I tell him: "You, more than anyone else, know that he's dead." And he says: "That's right, but after all, I'm only a public servant. The only legal way would be with a death certificate." And I tell him: "If the law is on your side, take advantage of it and bring a doctor who can make out the death certificate." And he, with his head lifted but without haughtiness, calmly too, but without the slightest show of weakness or confusion, says: "You're a respectable person and you know that it would be an abuse of authority." When I hear him I see that his brains are not addled so much by liquor as by cowardice.

Now I can see that the mayor shares the anger of the town. It's a feeling fed for ten years, ever since that stormy night when they brought the wounded men to the man's door and shouted to him (because he didn't open the door, he spoke from inside); they shouted to him: "Doctor, take care of these wounded men because there aren't enough doctors to go around," and still without opening (because the door stayed closed with the wounded lying in front of it). "You're the only doctor left. You have to do a charitable act"; and he replied (and he didn't open the door then either), imagined by the crowd to be standing in the middle of the living room, the lamp held high lighting up his hard yellow eyes: "I've forgotten everything I knew about all that. Take them somewhere else," and he kept the door closed (because from that time on the door was never opened again) while the anger grew, spread out, turned into a collective disease which gave no respite to Macondo for the rest of his life, and in every ear the sentence shouted that night—the one that condemned the doctor to rot behind these walls—continued echoing.

Ten years would still pass without his ever drinking the town water, haunted by the fear that it would be poisoned; feeding himself on the vegetables that he and his Indian mistress planted in the courtyard. Now the town feels that the time has come when they can deny him the pity that he denied the town ten years ago, and Macondo, which knows that he's dead (because everyone must have awakened with a lighter feeling this morning), is getting ready to enjoy that longed-for pleasure which everyone considers to be deserved. Their only desire is to smell the odor of organic decomposition behind the doors that he didn't open that other time.

Now I can begin to believe that nothing can help my promise in the face of the ferocity of a town and that I'm hemmed in, surrounded by the hatred and impatience of a band of resentful people. Even the Church has found a way to go against my determination. Father Ángel told me a moment ago: "I won't let them bury in consecrated ground a man who hanged himself after having lived sixty years without God. Our Lord would look upon you with good eyes too if you didn't carry out what won't be a work of charity but the sin of rebellion." I told him: "To bury the dead, as is written, is a work of charity." And Father Ángel said: "Yes. But in this case it's not up to us to do it, it's up to the sanitary authorities."

I came. I called the four Guajiros who were raised in my house. I made my daughter Isabel go with me. In that way the act becomes more family, more human, less personal and defiant than if I dragged the corpse to the cemetery through the streets of the town myself. I think Macondo is capable of doing anything after what I've seen happen in this century. But if they won't respect me, not even because I'm old, a Colonel of the Republic, and, to top it off, lame in body and sound in conscience, I hope that at least they'll respect my daughter because she's a woman. I'm not doing it for myself. Maybe not for the peace of the dead man either. Just to fulfill a sacred promise. If I brought Isabel along it wasn't out of cowardice but out of charity. She brought the child (and I can see that she did it for the same reason), and here we are now, the three of us, bearing the weight of this harsh emergency.

We got here a moment ago. I thought we'd find the body still hanging from the ceiling, but the men got here first, laid him on the bed, and almost shrouded him with the secret conviction that the affair wouldn't last more than an hour. When I arrive I hope they'll bring the coffin, I see my daughter and the child sitting in the corner and I examine the room, thinking that the doctor may have left something that will explain why he did it. The desk is open, full of a confusion of papers, none written by him. On the desk I see the same bound formulary that he brought to my house twenty-five years ago when he opened that enormous trunk which could have held the clothing of my whole family. But there was nothing else in the trunk except two cheap shirts, a set of false teeth that couldn't have been his for the simple reason that he still had his own, strong and complete, a portrait, and a formulary. I open the drawers and I find printed sheets of paper in all of them; just papers, old, dusty; and underneath, in the last drawer, the same false teeth that he brought twenty-five years ago, dusty, yellow from age and lack of use. On the small table beside the unlighted lamp there are several bundles of unopened newspapers. I examine them. They're written in French, the most recent ones three months old: *July, 1928.* And there are others, also unopened: *January, 1927; November, 1926.* And the oldest ones: *October, 1919.* I think: *It's been nine years, since one year after the sentence had been pronounced, that he hadn't opened the newspapers. Since that time he's given up the last thing that linked him to his land and his people.*

16

The men bring the coffin and lower the corpse into it. Then I remember the day twenty-five years ago when he arrived at my house and gave me the letter of recommendation, written in Panama and addressed to me by the Intendant General of the Atlantic Coast at the end of the great war, Colonel Aureliano Buendía. I search through various trifles in the darkness of the bottomless trunk. There's no clue in the other corner, only the same things he brought twenty-five years ago. I remember: *He had two cheap shirts, a set of teeth, a portrait, and that old bound formulary.* I go about gathering up these things before they close the coffin and I put them inside. The portrait is still at the bottom of the trunk, almost in the same place where it had been that time. It's the daguerreotype of a decorated officer. I throw the picture into the box. I throw in the false teeth and finally the formulary. When I finish I signal the men to close the coffin. I think: *Now he's on another trip. The most natural thing for him on his last trip is to take along the things that were with him on the next to the last one. At least that would seem to be the most natural.* And then I seem to see him, for the first time, comfortably dead.

I examine the room and I see that a shoe was forgotten on the bed. I signal my men again with the shoe in my hand and they lift up the lid at the precise moment when the train whistles, disappearing around the last bend in town. *It's two-thirty*, I think. *Two-thirty on September 12, 1928; almost the same hour of that day in 1903 when this man sat down for the first time at our table and asked for some grass to eat.* Adelaida asked him that time: "What kind of grass, doctor?" And he in his parsimonious ruminant voice, still touched by nasality: "Ordinary grass, ma'am. The kind that donkeys eat."

II.

The fact is that Meme isn't in the house and that probably no one could say exactly when she stopped living here. The last time I saw her was eleven years ago. She still had the little *botiquín* on this corner that had been imperceptibly modified by the needs of the neighbors until it had become a variety store. Everything in order, neatly arranged by the scrupulous and hardworking Meme, who spent her day sewing for the neighbors on one of the four Domestics that there were in town in those days or behind the counter attending to customers with that pleasant Indian way which she never lost and which was at the same time both open and reserved; a mixed-up combination of innocence and mistrust.

I hadn't seen Meme since the time she left our house, but actually I can't say exactly when she came here to live with the doctor on the corner or how she could have reached the extreme of degradation of becoming the mistress of a man who had refused her his services, in spite of everything and the fact that they shared my father's house, she as a foster child and he as a permanent guest. I learned from my stepmother that the doctor wasn't a good man, that he'd had a long argument with Papa, trying to convince him that what Meme had wasn't anything serious, not even leaving his room. In any case, even if what the Guajiro girl had was only a passing illness, he should have taken a look at her, if only because of the consideration with which he was treated in our house during the eight years he lived there.

I don't know how things happened. I just know that one morning Meme wasn't in the house anymore and he wasn't either. Then my stepmother had them close up his room and she didn't mention him again until years later when we were working on my wedding dress.

Three or four Sundays after she'd left our house, Meme went

18

to church, to eight o'clock mass, with a gaudy silk print dress and a ridiculous hat that was topped by a cluster of artificial flowers. She'd always been so simple when I saw her in our house, barefoot most of the time, so that the person who came into church that Sunday looked to me like a different Meme from the one we knew. She heard mass up front, among the ladies, stiff and affected under that pile of things she was wearing, which made her new and complicated, a showy newness made up of cheap things. She was kneeling down up front. And even the devotion with which she followed the mass was something new in her; even in the way she crossed herself there was something of that flowery and gaudy vulgarity with which she'd entered the church, puzzling people who had known her as a servant in our home and surprising those who'd never seen her.

I (I couldn't have been more than thirteen at the time) wondered what had brought on that transformation, why Meme had disappeared from our house and reappeared in church that Sunday dressed more like a Christmas tree than a lady, or with enough there to dress three women completely for Easter Sunday, and the Guajiro girl even had enough drippings and beads left over to dress a fourth one. When mass was over the men and women stopped by the door to watch her come out. They stood on the steps in a double row by the main door, and I think that there might even have been something secretly premeditated in that indolent and mockingly solemn way in which they were waiting, not saying a word until Meme came out the door, closed her eyes and opened them again in perfect rhythm to her seven-colored parasol. That was how she went between the double row of men and women, ridiculous in her high-heeled peacock disguise, until one of the men began to close the circle and Meme was in the middle, startled, confused, trying to smile with a smile of distinction that was as gaudy and false on her as her outfit. But when Meme came out, opened her parasol, and began to walk, Papa, who was next to me, pulled me toward the group. So when the men began closing the circle, my father opened a way out for Meme, who was hurriedly trying to get away. Papa took her by the arm without looking at the people there, and he led her through the center of the square with that haughty and challenging expression he puts on when he does something that other people don't agree with.

Some time passed before I found out that Meme had gone to live with the doctor as his mistress. In those days the shop was open and she still went to Mass like the finest of ladies, not bothered by what was thought or said, as if she'd forgotten what had happened that first Sunday. Still, two months later, she wasn't ever seen in church again.

I remember the doctor when he was staying at our house. I remember his black and twisted mustache and his way of looking at women with his lustful, greedy dog eyes. But I remember that I never got close to him, maybe because I thought of him as the strange animal that stayed seated at the table after everyone had gotten up and ate the same kind of grass that donkeys eat. During Papa's illness three years ago, the doctor didn't leave his corner the same as he hadn't left it one single time after the night he refused to attend to the wounded men, just as six years before that he'd denied the woman who two days later would be his concubine. The small house had been shut up before the town passed sentence on the doctor. But I do know that Meme was still living here for several months or several years after the store was closed. It must have been much later when people found out that she'd disappeared, because that was what the anonymous note tacked on this door said. According to that note, the doctor had murdered his mistress and buried her in the garden because he was afraid the town would use her to poison him. But I'd seen Meme before I was married. It was eleven years ago, when I was coming back from rosary and the Guajiro woman came to the door of her shop and said to me in her jolly and somewhat ironic way: "Chabela, you're getting married and you didn't even tell me."

* * *

"Yes," I tell him, "that's how it must have been." Then I tug
on the noose, where on one of the ends the living flesh of the
newly cut rope can be seen. I retie the knot my men had cut in
order to take the body down and I toss one of the ends over the
beam until the noose is hanging, held with enough strength to
contribute many deaths just like this man's. While he fans himself with his hat, his face altered by shortness of breath and
liquor, looking at the noose, calculating its strength, he says: "A
noose as thin as that couldn't possibly have held his body." And
I tell him: "That same rope held up his hammock for many years."
And he pulls a chair over, hands me his hat, and hangs from the
noose by his hands, his face flushed by the effort. Then he stands
on the chair again, looking at the end of the hanging rope. He
says: "Impossible. That noose doesn't reach down to my neck."
And then I can see that he's being illogical deliberately, looking
for ways to hold off the burial.

I look at him straight in the face, scrutinizing him. I tell him:
"Didn't you ever notice that he was at least a head taller than you?"
And he turns to look at the coffin. He says: "All the same, I'm not
sure he did it with this noose."

I'm sure it was done that way. And he knows it too, but he
has a scheme for wasting time because he's afraid of compromising
himself. His cowardice can be seen in the way he moves around
in no direction. A double and contradictory cowardice: to hold off
the ceremony and to set it up. Then, when he gets to the coffin,
he turns on his heels, looks at me, and says: "I'd have to see him
hanging to be convinced."

I would have done it. I would have told my men to open the
coffin and put the hanged man back up again the way he was
until a moment ago. But it would be too much for my daughter.
It would be too much for the child, and she shouldn't have
brought him. Even though it upsets me to treat a dead man that
way, offending defenseless flesh, disturbing a man who's at rest
for the first time; even though the act of moving a corpse who's

lying peacefully and deservedly in his coffin is against my principles, I'd hang him up again just to see how far this man will go. But it's impossible. And I tell him so: "You can rest assured that I won't tell them to do that. If you want to, hang him up yourself, and you can be responsible for what happens. Remember that we don't know how long he's been dead."

He hasn't moved. He's still beside the coffin, looking at me, then looking at Isabel and then at the child, and then at the coffin again. Suddenly his expression becomes somber and menacing. He says: "You must know what can happen because of this." And I can see what he means by his threat. I tell him: "Of course I do. I'm a responsible person." And he, his arms folded now, sweating, walking toward me with studied and comical movements that pretend to be threatening, says: "May I ask you how you found out that this man had hanged himself last night?"

I wait for him to get in front of me. I remain motionless, looking at him until my face is hit by his hot, harsh breath, until he stops, his arms still folded, moving his hat behind one armpit. Then I say to him: "When you ask me that in an official capacity, I'll be very pleased to give you an answer." He stands facing me in the same position. When I speak to him he doesn't show the least bit of surprise or upset. He says: "Naturally, colonel, I'm asking you officially."

I'll give him all the rope he wants. I'm sure that no matter how much he tries to twist it, he'll have to give in to an ironclad position, but one that's patient and calm. I tell him: "These men cut the body down because I couldn't let it stay hanging there until you decided to come. I told you to come two hours ago and you took all this time to walk two blocks."

He still doesn't move. I face him, resting on my cane, leaning forward a little. I say: "In the second place, he was my friend." Before I can finish speaking he smiles ironically, but without changing position, throwing his thick and sour breath into my face. He says: "It's the easiest thing in the world, isn't it?" And

22

suddenly he stops smiling. He says: "So you knew this man was going to hang himself."

Tranquil, patient, convinced that he's only going on like that to complicate things, I say to him: "I repeat. The first thing I did when I found out he'd hanged himself was to go to your place and that was two hours ago." And as if I'd asked him a question and not stated something, he says: "I was having lunch." And I say to him: "I know. I even think you took time out for a siesta."

Then he doesn't know what to say. He moves back. He looks at Isabel sitting beside the child. He looks at the men and finally at me. But his expression is changed now. He seems to be looking for something to occupy his thought for a moment. He turns his back on me, goes to where the policeman is, and tells him something. The policeman nods and leaves the room.

Then he comes back and takes my arm. He says: "I'd like to talk to you in the other room, colonel." Now his voice has changed completely. It's tense and disturbed now. And while I walk into the next room, feeling the uncertain pressure of his hand on my arm, I'm taken with the idea that I know what he's going to tell me.

This room, unlike the other one, is big and cool. The light from the courtyard flows into it. In here I can see his disturbed eyes, the smile that doesn't match the expression of his eyes. I can hear his voice saying: "Colonel, maybe we can settle this another way." And without giving him time to finish, I ask him: "How much?" And then he becomes a different man.

Meme had brought out a plate with jelly and two salt rolls, the kind that she'd learned to make from my mother. The clock had struck nine. Meme was sitting opposite me in the back of the store and was eating listlessly, as if the jelly and rolls were only something to hold together the visit. I understood that and let her lose herself in her labyrinths, sink into the past with that nostalgic and sad enthusiasm that in the light of the oil lamp burning on the counter made her look more withered and old than the day she'd come into church wearing the hat and high heels. It was obvious that Meme felt like recalling things that night. And while she was doing it, one had the impression that over the past years she'd held herself back in some unique and timeless static age and that as she recalled things that night she was putting her personal time into motion again and beginning to go through her long-postponed aging process.

Meme was stiff and somber, talking about the picturesque and feudal splendor of our family during the last years of the previous century, before the great war. Meme recalled my mother. She recalled her that night when I was coming back from church and she told me in her somewhat mocking and ironic way: "Chabela, you're getting married and you didn't even tell me." Those were precisely the days when I'd wanted my mother and was trying to bring her back more strongly in my memory. "She was the living picture of you," she said. And I really believed it. I was sitting across from the Indian woman, who spoke with an accent mixed with precision and vagueness, as if there was a lot of incredible legend in what she was recalling but also as if she was recalling it in good faith and even with the conviction that the passage of time had changed legend into reality that was remote but hard to forget. She spoke to me about the journey my parents had made during the war, about the rough pilgrimage that would end with their settling in Macondo. My parents were fleeing the hazards of war and looking for a prosperous and tranquil bend in the road to settle down in, and they heard about the golden calf and came looking for it in what was then a town in formation, founded by several refugee families whose members were as careful about the preservation of their traditions and religious practices as the fattening of their hogs. Macondo was my parents' promised land, peace, and the Parchment. Here they found the appropriate spot to rebuild the house that a few years later would be a country mansion with three stables and two guest rooms. Meme recalled the details without repentance, and spoke about the most extravagant things with an irrepressible desire to live them again or with the pain that came from the fact that she would never live them again. There was no suffering or privation on the journey, she said. Even the horses slept under mosquito netting, not because my father was a spendthrift or a madman, but because my mother had a strange sense of charity, of humanitarian feelings, and thought that the eyes of God would be just as pleased with the act of protecting an animal from the mosquitoes as protecting a man. Their wild and burdensome cargo was everywhere; the trunks full of clothing of people who had died before they'd been on earth, ancestors who couldn't have been found twenty fathoms under the earth; boxes full of kitchen utensils that hadn't been used for a long time and had belonged to my parents' most distant relatives (my father and mother were first cousins), and even a trunk filled with the images of saints, which they used to reconstruct their family altar everywhere they stopped. It was a strange carnival procession with horses and hens and the four Guajiro Indians (Meme's companions) who had grown up in the house and followed my parents all through the region like trained circus animals.

Meme recalled things with sadness. One had the impression that she considered the passage of time a personal loss, as if she noticed in that heart of hers, lacerated by memories, that if time hadn't passed she'd still be on that pilgrimage, which must have been a punishment for my parents, but which was a kind of lark for the children, with strange sights like that of horses under mosquito netting.

Then everything began to go backward, she said. Their arrival in the newborn village of Macondo during the last days of the century was that of a devastated family, still bound to a recent splendid past, disorganized by the war. The Indian woman recalled my mother's arrival in town, sidesaddle on a mule, pregnant, her face green and malarial and her feet disabled by swelling.

Perhaps the seeds of resentment were maturing in my father's soul but he came ready to sink roots against wind and tide while he waited for my mother to bear the child that had been growing in her womb during the crossing and was progressively bringing death to her as the time of birth drew near.

The light of the lamp outlined her profile. Meme, with her stiff Indian expression, her hair straight and thick like a horse's mane or tail, looked like a sitting idol, green and spectral in the small hot room behind the store, speaking the way an idol would have if it had set out to recall its ancient earthly existence. I'd never been close to her, but that night, after that sudden and spontaneous show of intimacy, I felt that I was tied to her by bonds tighter than those of blood.

Suddenly, during one of Meme's pauses, I heard coughing in the next room, in this very bedroom where I am now with the child and my father. It was a short, dry cough, followed by a clearing of the throat, and then I heard the unmistakable sound that a man makes when he rolls over in bed. Meme stopped talking at once, and a gloomy, silent cloud darkened her face. I'd forgotten about him. During the time I was there (it was around ten o'clock) I had felt as if the Guajiro woman and I were alone in the house. Then the tension of the atmosphere changed. I felt fatigue in the arm with which I'd been holding the plate with the jelly and rolls, without tasting any. I leaned over and said: "He's awake." She, expressionless now, cold and completely indifferent, said: "He'll be awake until dawn." And suddenly I understood the disillusionment that could be seen in Meme when she recalled the past of our house. Our lives had changed, the times were good and Macondo was a bustling town where there was even enough money to squander on Saturday nights, but Meme was living tied to a past that had been better. While they were shearing the golden calf outside, inside, in the back of the store, her life was sterile, anonymous, all day behind the counter and spending the night with a man who didn't sleep until dawn, who spent his time walking about the house, pacing, looking at her greedily with those lustful dog eyes that I've never been able to forget. It saddened me to think of Meme with that man who refused his services one night and went on being a hardened animal, without bitterness or compassion, all day long in ceaseless roaming through the house, enough to drive the most balanced person out of his mind.

Recovering the tone of my voice, knowing that he was in his room, awake, maybe opening his lustful dog eyes every time our words were heard in the rear of the store, I tried to give a different turn to the conversation.

"How's business been for you?" I asked.

Meme smiled. Her laugh was sad and taciturn, seeming detached from any feeling of the moment, like something she kept in the cupboard and took out only when she had to, using it with no feeling of ownership, as if the infrequency of her smiles had made her forget the normal way to use them. "There it is," she said, moving her head in an ambiguous way, and she was silent, abstract again. Then I understood that it was time for me to leave. I handed Meme the plate without giving any explanation as to why it was untouched, and I watched her get up and put it on the counter. She looked at me from there and repeated: "You're the living picture of her." I must have been sitting against the light before, clouded by it as it came in the opposite direction and Meme couldn't see my face while she'd been talking. Then when she got up to put the plate on the counter she saw me frontward, from behind the lamp, and that was why she said: "You're the living picture of her." And she came back to sit down.

Then she began to recall the days when my mother had arrived in Macondo. She'd gone directly from the mule to a rocking chair and stayed seated for three months, not moving, taking her food listlessly. Sometimes they would bring her lunch and she'd sit halfway through the afternoon with the plate in her hand, rigid, not rocking, her feet resting on a chair, feeling death growing inside of them until someone would come and take the plate from her hands. When the day came, the labor pains drew her out of her abandonment and she stood up by herself, although they had to help her walk the twenty steps between the porch and the bedroom, martyrized by the occupation of a death that had taken her over during nine months of silent suffering. Her crossing from the rocker to the bed had all the pain, bitterness, and penalties that had been absent during the journey taken a few months before, but she arrived where she knew she had to arrive before she fulfilled the last act of her life.

My father seemed desperate over my mother's death, Meme said. But according to what he himself said afterward when he was alone in the house, "No one trusts the morality of a home where the man doesn't have a legitimate wife by his side." And since he'd read somewhere that when a loved one dies we should set out a bed of jasmine to remember her every night, he planted a vine against the courtyard wall, and a year later, in a second marriage, he was wedded to Adelaida, my stepmother.

Sometimes I thought that Meme was going to cry while she was speaking. But she remained firm, satisfied at expiating the loss of having been happy once and having stopped being so by her own free will. Then she smiled. Then she relaxed in her chair and became completely human. It was as if she'd drawn up mental accounts of her grief when she leaned forward and saw that she still had a favorable balance in good memories left, and then she smiled with her old wide and teasing friendliness. She said that the other thing had started five years later, when she came into the dining room where my father was having lunch and told him: "Colonel, colonel, there's a stranger to see you in your office."

III.

Behind the church, on the other side of the street, there was once a lot with no trees. That was toward the end of the last century, when we came to Macondo and they hadn't started to build the church yet. It was a dry, bald plot of land where the children played after school. Later on, when construction on the church began, they set up four beams to one side of the lot and it could be seen that the encircled space was just right for building a hut. Which they did. Inside they kept the materials for the construction of the church.

When the work on the church came to an end, someone finished putting adobe on the walls of the small hut and opened a door in the rear wall, which faced the small, bare, stony plot where there was not even a trace of an aloe bush. A year later the small hut was finished, big enough for two people. Inside there was a smell of quicklime. That was the only pleasant odor that had been smelled for a long time inside that enclosure and the only agreeable one that would be smelled ever after. When they had whitewashed the walls, the same hand that had completed the construction ran a bar across the inside door and put a padlock on the street door.

The hut had no owner. No one worried about making his rights effective over either the lot or the construction materials. When the first parish priest arrived he put up with one of the well-to-do families in Macondo. Then he was transferred to a different parish. But during those days (and possibly before the first priest had left) a woman with a child at her breast had occupied the hut, and no one knew when she had come, nor from where, nor how she had managed to open the door. There was an earthen crock in a corner, black and green with moss, and a jar hanging from a nail. But there wasn't any more whitewash left on the walls. In the yard a crust of earth hardened by the rain had formed over the stones. The woman built a network of branches to protect herself from the sun. And since she had no means to put a roof of palm leaves, tile, or zinc on it, she planted a grapevine beside the branches and hung a clump of *sábila* and a loaf of bread by the street door to protect herself against evil thoughts.

When the coming of the new priest was announced in 1903, the woman was still living in the hut with her child. Half of the population went out to the highway to wait for the priest to arrive. The rural band was playing sentimental pieces until a boy came running, panting to the point of bursting, saying that the priest's mule was at the last bend in the road. Then the musicians changed their position and began to play a march. The person assigned to give the welcoming speech climbed up on an improvised platform and waited for the priest to appear so that he could begin his greeting. But a moment later the martial tune was suspended, the orator got down off the table, and the astonished multitude watched a stranger pass by, riding a mule whose haunches carried the largest trunk ever seen in Macondo. The man went by on his way into town without looking at anyone. Even if the priest had been dressed in civilian clothes for the trip, it would never have occurred to anyone that the bronzed traveler in military leggings was a priest dressed in civilian clothes.

And, in fact, he wasn't, because at that very same moment, along the shortcut on the other side of town, people saw a strange priest coming along, fearfully thin, with a dry and stretched-out face, astride a mule, his cassock lifted up to his knees, and protected from the sun by a faded and run-down umbrella. In the neighborhood of the church the priest asked where the parish house was, and he must have asked someone who didn't have the least idea of anything, because the answer he got was: "It's the hut behind the church, father." The woman had gone out, but the child was playing inside behind the half-open door. The priest dismounted, rolled a swollen suitcase over to the hut. It was unlocked, just barely held together by a leather strap that was different from the hide of the suitcase itself, and after he examined the hut, he brought up the mule and tied it in the yard in the shade of the grape leaves. Then he opened up the suitcase, took out a hammock that must have been the same age and had seen the same use as the umbrella, hung it diagonally across the

30

hut, from beam to beam, took off his boots, and tried to sleep, unconcerned about the child, who was looking at him with great frightened eyes.

When the woman returned she must have felt disconcerted by the strange presence of the priest, whose face was so inexpressive that it was in no way different from the skull of a cow. The woman must have tiptoed across the room. She must have dragged her folding cot to the door, made a bundle of her clothes and the child's rags, and left the hut without even bothering about the crock and the jar, because an hour later, when the delegation went back through town in the opposite direction preceded by the band, which was playing its martial air in the midst of a crowd of boys who had skipped school, they found the priest alone in the hut, stretched out in his hammock in a carefree way, his cassock unbuttoned and his shoes off. Someone must have brought the news to the main road, but it occurred to no one to ask what the priest was doing in that hut. They must have thought that he was related to the woman in some way, just as she must have abandoned the hut because she thought that the priest had orders to occupy it, or that it was church property, or simply out of fear that they would ask her why she had lived for more than two years in a hut that didn't belong to her without paying any rent or without anyone's permission. Nor did it occur to the delegation to ask for any explanation, neither then nor any time after, because the priest wouldn't accept any speeches. He laid the presents on the floor and limited himself to greeting the men and women coldly and quickly, because according to what he said, he hadn't shut his eyes all night.

The delegation dissolved in the face of that cold reception by the strangest priest they'd ever seen. They noticed how his face looked like the skull of a cow, with closely cropped gray hair, and he didn't have any lips, but a horizontal opening that seemed not to have been in the place of his mouth since birth but made later on by a quick and unique knife. But that very afternoon they realized that he looked like someone. And before dawn everyone knew who it was. They remembered having seen him with a sling and a stone, naked, but wearing shoes and a hat, during the time when Macondo was a humble refugee village. The veterans remembered his activities in the civil war of '85. They remembered that he had been a colonel at the age of seventeen and that he was intrepid, hardheaded, and against the government. But nothing had been heard of him again in Macondo until that day when he returned home to take over the parish. Very few remembered his given name. On the other hand, most of the veterans remembered the one his mother had put on him (because he was willful and rebellious) and that it was the same one that his comrades in arms would call him by later on. They all called him the Pup. And that was what he was always called in Macondo until the hour of his death:

"Pup, Puppy."

So it was that this man came to our house on the same day and almost at the same hour that the Pup reached Macondo. The former along the main road, unexpected and with no one having the slightest notion of his name or profession; the priest by the shortcut, while the whole town was waiting for him on the main road.

I returned home after the reception. We had just sat down to the table—a little later than usual—when Meme came over to tell me: "Colonel, colonel, colonel, there's a stranger to see you in your office." I said: "Tell him to come in." And Meme said: "He's in the office and says that he has to see you at once." Adelaida stopped feeding soup to Isabel (she couldn't have been more than five at the time) and went to take care of the newcomer. A moment later she came back, visibly worried:

"He's pacing back and forth in the office," she said.

I saw her walk behind the candlesticks. Then she began to feed Isabel her soup again. "You should have had him come in," I said, still eating. And she said: "That's what I was going to do. But he was pacing back and forth in the office when I got there and said good afternoon, but he didn't answer me because he was looking at the leather dancing girl on the shelf. And when I was about to say good afternoon again, he wound up the dancing girl, put her on the desk, and watched her dance. I don't know whether it was the music that prevented him from hearing when I said good afternoon again, but I stood there opposite the desk, where he was leaning over watching the dancing girl, who was still wound up a little." Adelaida was feeding Isabel her soup. I said to her: "He must be very interested in the toy." And she, still feeding Isabel her soup: "He was pacing back and forth in the office, but then, when he saw the dancing girl, he took her down as if he knew beforehand what it was for, as if he knew how it worked. He was winding it up when I said good afternoon to him for the first time, before the music began to play. Then he put it on the desk and stood there watching it, but without smiling, as if he weren't interested in the dance but in the mechanism."

They never announced anyone to me. Visitors came almost every day: travelers we knew, who left their animals in the stable and came in with complete confidence, with the familiarity of one who always expects to find an empty place at our table. I told Adelaida: "He must have a message or something." And she said: "In any case, he's acting very strangely. He's watching the dancing girl until it runs down and in the meantime I'm standing across the desk without knowing what to say to him, because I knew that he wouldn't answer me as long as the music was playing. Then, when the dancing girl gave the little leap she always gives when she runs down, he was still standing there looking at her with curiosity, leaning over the desk but not sitting down. Then he looked at me and I realized that he knew I was in the office but that he hadn't worried about me because he wanted to know how long the dancing girl would keep on dancing. I didn't say good afternoon to him again, but I smiled when he looked at me because I saw that he had huge eyes, with yellow pupils, and they look at a person's whole body all at the same time. When I smiled at him he remained serious, but he nodded his head very formally and said: 'The colonel. It's the colonel I have to see.' He has a deep voice, as if he could speak with his mouth closed. As if he were a ventriloquist."

She was feeding Isabel her soup, and she said: "At first he was pacing back and forth in the office." Then I understood that the stranger had made an uncommon impression on her and that she had a special interest in my taking care of him. Nevertheless, I kept on eating lunch while she fed Isabel her soup and spoke. She said: "Then, when he said he wanted to see the colonel, what I told him was 'Please come into the dining room,' and he straightened up where he was, with the dancing girl in his hand. Then he raised his head and became as rigid and firm as a soldier, I think, because he's wearing high boots and a suit of ordinary cloth, with the shirt buttoned up to his neck. I didn't know what to say when he didn't answer anything and was quiet, with the toy in his hand, as if he were waiting for me to leave the office in order to wind it up again. That was when he suddenly reminded me of someone, when I realized that he was a military man."

And I told her: "So you think it's something serious." I looked at her over the candlesticks. She wasn't looking at me. She was feeding Isabel her soup. She said:

"When I got there he was pacing back and forth in the office and so I couldn't see his face. But then when he stood in the back he had his head held so high and his eyes were so fixed that I think he's a military man, and I said to him: 'You want to see the colonel in private, is that it?' And he nodded. Then I came to tell you that he looks like someone, or rather, that he's the same person that he looks like, although I can't explain how he got here."

I kept on eating, but I was looking at her over the candlesticks. She stopped feeding Isabel her soup. She said:

"I'm sure it's not a message. I'm sure it's not that he looks like someone but that he's the same person he looks like. I'm sure, rather, that he's a military man. He's got a black pointed mustache and a face like copper. He's wearing high boots and I'm sure that it's not that he looks like someone but that he's the same person he looks like."

She was speaking in a level tone, monotonous and persistent. It was hot and maybe for that reason I began to feel irritated. I said to her: "So, who does he look like?" And she said: "When he was pacing back and forth in the office I couldn't see his face, but later on." And I, irritated with the monotony and persistence of her words: "All right, all right, I'll go to see him when I finish my lunch." And she, feeding Isabel her soup again: "At first I couldn't see his face because he was pacing back and forth in the office. But then when I said to him: 'Please come in,' he stood there silent beside the wall with the dancing girl in his hand. That was when I remembered who he looks like and I came to tell you. He has huge, indiscreet eyes, and when I turned to leave I felt that he was looking right at my legs."

She suddenly fell silent. In the dining room the metallic tinkle of the spoon kept vibrating. I finished my lunch and folded the napkin under my plate.

At that moment from the office I heard the festive music of the wind-up toy.

IV.

In the kitchen of the house there's an old carved wooden chair without crosspieces and my grandfather puts his shoes to dry next to the stove on its broken seat.

Tobías, Abraham, Gilberto, and I left school at this time yesterday and we went to the plantations with a sling, a big hat to hold the birds, and a new knife. On the way I was remembering the useless chair placed in the kitchen corner, which at one time was used for visitors and which now is used by the dead man who sits down every night with his hat on to look at the ashes in the cold stove.

Tobías and Gilberto were walking toward the end of the dark nave. Since it had rained during the morning, their shoes slipped on the muddy grass. One of them was whistling, and his hard, firm whistle echoed in the vegetable cavern the way it does when someone starts to sing inside a barrel. Abraham was bringing up the rear with me. He with his sling and the stone, ready to shoot. I with my open knife.

Suddenly the sun broke the roof of tight, hard leaves and a body of light fell winging down onto the grass like a live bird. "Did you see it?" Abraham asked. I looked ahead and saw Gilberto and Tobías at the end of the nave. "It's not a bird," I said. "It's the sun that's just come out strong."

When they got to the bank they began to get undressed and gave strong kicks in that twilight water, which didn't seem to wet their skin. "There hasn't been a single bird all afternoon," Abraham said. "There aren't any birds after it rains," I said. And I believed it myself then. Abraham began to laugh. His laugh is foolish and simple and it makes a sound like that of a thread of water from a spigot. He got undressed. "I'll take the knife into the water and fill the hat with fish," he said.

Abraham was naked in front of me with his hand open, waiting for the knife. I didn't answer right away. I held the knife tight and I felt its clean and tempered steel in my hand. *I'm not going to give him the knife*, I thought. And I told him: "I'm not going to give you the knife. I only got it yesterday and I'm going to keep it all afternoon." Abraham kept his hand out. Then I told him:

"*Incomploruto*."

Abraham understood me. He's the only one who can understand my words. "All right," he said and walked toward the water through the hardened, sour air. He said: "Start getting undressed and we'll wait for you on the rock." And he said it as he dove in and reappeared shining like an enormous silver-plated fish, as if the water had turned to liquid as it came in contact with him.

I stayed on the bank, lying on the warm mud. When I opened the knife again I stopped looking at Abraham and lifted my eyes up straight toward the other side, up toward the trees, toward the furious dusk where the sky had the monstrous awfulness of a burning stable.

"Hurry up," Abraham said from the other side. Tobías was whistling on the edge of the rock. Then I thought: *I'm not going swimming today. Tomorrow.*

On the way back Abraham hid behind the hawthorns. I was going to follow him, but he told me: "Don't come back here. I'm doing something." I stayed outside, sitting on the dead leaves in the road, watching a single swallow that was tracing a curve in the sky. I said:

"There's only one swallow this afternoon."

Abraham didn't answer right away. He was silent behind the hawthorns, as if he couldn't hear me, as if he were reading. His silence was deep and concentrated, full of a hidden strength. After a long silence he sighed. Then he said:

"Swallows."

I told him again: "There's only one swallow this afternoon." Abraham was still behind the hawthorns but I couldn't tell anything about him. He was silent and drawn in, but his silence wasn't static. It was a desperate and impetuous immobility. After a moment he said:

"Only one? Ah, yes. You're right, you're right."

I didn't say anything then. Behind the hawthorns, he was the one who began to move. Sitting on the leaves, I could hear the sound of other dead leaves under his feet from where he was. Then he was silent again, as if he'd gone away. Then he breathed deeply and asked:

"What did you say?"

I told him again: "There's only one swallow this afternoon." And while I was saying it I saw the curved wing tracing circles in the sky of incredible blue. "He's flying high," I said.

Abraham replied at once:

"Ah, yes, of course. That must be why then."

He came out from behind the hawthorns, buttoning up his pants. He looked up toward where the swallow was still tracing circles, and, still not looking at me, he said:

"What were you telling me a while back about the swallows?"

That held us up. When we got back the lights in town were on. I ran into the house and on the veranda I came on the fat, blind women with the twins of Saint Jerome who every Tuesday have come to sing for my grandfather since before I was born, according to what my mother says.

All night I was thinking that today we'd get out of school again and go to the river, but not with Gilberto and Tobías. I want to go alone with Abraham, to see the shine of his stomach when he dives and comes up again like a metal fish. All night long I've wanted to go back with him, alone in the darkness of the green tunnel, to brush his thigh as we walk along. Whenever I do that I feel as if someone is biting me with soft nibbles and my skin creeps.

If this man who's come to talk to my grandfather in the other room comes back in a little while maybe we can be home before four o'clock. Then I'll go to the river with Abraham.

He stayed on to live at our house. He occupied one of the rooms off the veranda, the one that opens onto the street, because I thought it would be convenient, for I knew that a man of his type wouldn't be comfortable in the small hotel in town. He put a sign on the door (it was still there until a few years ago when they whitewashed the house, written in pencil in his own hand),

and on the following week we had to bring in new chairs to take care of the demands of his numerous patients.

After he gave me the letter from Colonel Aureliano Buendía, our conversation in the office went on so long that Adelaida had no doubts but that it was a matter of some high military official on an important mission, and she set the table as if for a holiday. We spoke about Colonel Buendía, his premature daughter, and his wild firstborn son. The conversation had not gone on too long when I gathered that the man knew the Intendant General quite well and that he had enough regard for him to warrant his confidence. When Meme came to tell us that dinner was served, I thought that my wife had improvised some things in order to take care of the newcomer. But a far cry from improvisation was that splendid table served on the new cloth, on the chinaware destined exclusively for family dinners on Christmas and New Year's Day.

Adelaida was solemnly sitting up straight at one end of the table in a velvet dress closed up to the neck, the one that she wore before our marriage to attend to family business in the city. Adelaida had more refined customs than we did, a certain social experience which, since our marriage, had begun to influence the ways of my house. She had put on the family medallion, the one that she displayed at moments of exceptional importance, and all of her, just like the table, the furniture, the air that was breathed in the dining room, brought on a severe feeling of composure and cleanliness. When we reached the parlor, the man, who was always so careless in his dress and manners, must have felt ashamed and out of place, for he checked the button on his shirt as if he were wearing a tie, and a slight nervousness could be noticed in his unworried and strong walk. I can remember nothing with such precision as that instant in which we went into the dining room and I myself felt dressed too domestically for a table like the one Adelaida had prepared.

There was beef and game on the plates. Everything the same, however, as at our regular meals at that time, except for the presentation on the new china, between the newly polished candlesticks, which was spectacular and different from the norm. In spite of the fact that my wife knew that we would be having only one visitor, she had set eight places, and the bottle of wine in the center was an exaggerated manifestation of the diligence with which she had prepared the homage for the man whom, from the first moment, she had confused with a distinguished military functionary. Never before had I seen in my house an environment more loaded with unreality.

Adelaida's clothing would have been ridiculous had it not been for her hands (they were beautiful, really, and overly white), which balanced, along with her regal distinction, the falsity and arrangement of her appearance. It was when he checked the button on his shirt and hesitated that I got ahead of myself and said: "My second wife, *doctor*." A cloud darkened Adelaida's face and turned it strange and gloomy. She didn't budge from where she was, her hand held out, smiling, but no longer with the air of ceremonious stiffness that she had had when we came into the dining room.

The newcomer clicked his heels like a military man, touched his forehead with the tips of his extended fingers, and then walked over to where she was.

"Yes, ma'am," he said. But he didn't pronounce any name.

Only when I saw him clumsily shake Adelaida's hand did I become aware that his manners were vulgar and common.

He sat at the other end of the table, between the new crystal ware, between the candlesticks. His disarrayed presence stood out like a soup stain on the tablecloth.

Adelaida poured the wine. Her emotion from the beginning had been changed into a passive nervousness that seemed to say: *It's all right, everything will be done the way it was laid out, but you owe me an explanation.*

And it was after she served the wine and sat down at the other end of the table, while Meme got ready to serve the plates, that he leaned back in his chair, rested his hands on the tablecloth, and said with a smile:

"Look, miss, just start boiling a little grass and bring that to me as if it were soup."

Meme didn't move. She tried to laugh, but she couldn't get it out; instead she turned toward Adelaida. Then she, smiling too, but visibly upset, asked him: "What kind of grass, doctor?" And he, in his parsimonious ruminant voice:

"Ordinary grass, ma'am. The kind that donkeys eat."

V.

There's a moment when siesta time runs dry. Even the secret, hidden, minute activity of the insects ceases at that precise instant; the course of nature comes to a halt; creation stumbles on the brink of chaos and women get up, drooling, with the flower of the embroidered pillowcase on their cheeks, suffocated by temperature and rancor; and they think: *It's still Wednesday in Macondo*. And then they go back to huddling in the corner, splicing sleep to reality, and they come to an agreement, weaving the whispering as if it were an immense flat surface of thread stitched in common by all the women in town.

If inside time had the same rhythm as that outside, we would be in the bright sunlight now, in the middle of the street with the coffin. It would be later outside: it would be nighttime. It would be a heavy September night with a moon and women sitting in their courtyards chatting under the green light, and in the street, us, the renegades, in the full sunlight of this thirsty September. No one will interfere with the ceremony. I expected the mayor to be inflexible in his determination to oppose it and that we could have gone home; the child to school and my father to his clogs, the washbasin under his head dripping with cool water, and on the left-hand side his pitcher with iced lemonade. But now it's different. My father has once more been sufficiently persuasive to impose his point of view on what I thought at first was the mayor's irrevocable determination. Outside the town is bustling, given over to the work of a long, uniform, and pitiless whispering; and the clean street, without a shadow on the clean dust, virgin since the last wind swept away the tracks of the last ox. And it's a town with no one, with closed houses, where nothing is heard in the rooms except the dull bubbling of words pronounced by evil hearts. And in the room, the sitting child, stiff, looking at his shoes; slowly his eyes go to the lamp, then to the newspapers, again to his shoes, and now quickly to the hanged man, his bitten tongue, his glassy dog eyes that have no lust now; a dog with no appetite, dead. The child looks at him, thinks about the hanged man lying underneath the boards; he has a sad expression and then everything changes: a stool comes out by the door of the barbershop and inside the small altar with the mirror, the powder, and the scented water. The hand becomes freckled and large, it's no longer the hand of my son, it's been changed into a large, deft hand that coldly, with calculated parsimony, begins to strop the razor while the ear hears the metallic buzzing of the tempered blade and the head thinks: *Today they'll be coming earlier because it's Wednesday in Macondo*. And then they come, sit on the chairs in the shade and the coolness of the threshold, grim, squinting, their legs crossed, their hands folded over their knees, biting on the tips of their cigars; looking, talking about the same thing, watching the closed window across from them, the silent house with Señora Rebeca inside. She forgot something too: she forgot to disconnect the fan and she's going through the rooms with screened windows, nervous, stirred up, going through the knick-knacks of her sterile and tormented widowhood in order to be convinced by her sense of touch that she won't have died before the hour of burial comes. She's opening and closing the doors of her rooms, waiting for the patriarchal clock to rise up out of its siesta and reward her senses by striking three. All this, while the child's expression ends and he goes back to being hard and stiff, not even delaying half the time a woman needs to give the last stitch on the machine and raise her head full of curlers. Before the child goes back to being upright and pensive, the woman has rolled the machine to the corner of the veranda, and the men have bitten their cigars twice while they watch a complete passage of the razor across the cowhide; and Águeda, the cripple, makes a last effort to awaken her dead knees; and Señora Rebeca turns the lock again and thinks: *Wednesday in Macondo. A good day to bury the devil.* But then the child moves again and there's a new change in time. When something moves you can tell that time has passed. Not till then. Until something moves time is eternal, the sweat, the shirt drooling on the skin, and the unbribable and icy dead man, behind his bitten tongue. That's why time doesn't pass for the hanged man: because even if the child's hand moves, he doesn't know it. And while the dead man doesn't know it (because the child is still moving his hand), Águeda must have gone through another bead on her rosary; Señora Rebeca, lounging in her folding chair, is perplexed, watching the clock remain fixed on the edge of the imminent minute, and Águeda has had time (even though the second hasn't passed on Señora Rebeca's clock) to go through another bead on her rosary and think: *I'd do that if I could get to Father Ángel.* Then the child's hand descends and the razor makes a motion on the strop and one of the men sitting in the coolness of the threshold says: "It must be around three-thirty, right?" Then the hand stops. A dead clock on the brink of the next minute once more, the razor halted once more in the limits of its own steel; and Águeda still waiting for a new movement of the hand to stretch her legs and burst into the sacristy with her arms open, her knees moving again, saying: "Father, Father." And Father Ángel, prostrate in the child's immobility, running his tongue over his lips and the viscous taste of the meatball nightmare, seeing Águeda, would then say: "This is undoubtedly a miracle," and then, rolling about again in the sweaty, drooly drowsiness: "In any case, Águeda, this is no time for saying a mass for the souls in Purgatory." But the new movement is frustrated, my father comes into the room and the two times are reconciled; the two halves become adjusted, consolidate, and Señora Rebeca's clock realizes that it's been caught between the child's parsimony and the widow's impatience, and then it yawns, confused, dives into the prodigious quiet of the moment and comes out afterward dripping with liquid time, with exact and rectified time, and it leans forward and says with ceremonious dignity: "It's exactly two forty-seven." And my father, who, without knowing it, has broken the paralysis of the instant, says: "You're lost in the clouds, daughter." And I say: "Do you think something might happen?" And he, sweating, smiling: "At least I'm sure that the rice will be burned and the milk spilled in lots of houses."

The coffin's closed now, but I can remember the dead man's face. I've got it so clearly that if I look at the wall I can see his open eyes, his tight gray cheeks that are like damp earth, his bitten tongue to one side of his mouth. This gives me a burning, restless feeling. Maybe if my pants weren't so tight on one side of my leg.

My grandfather's sat down beside my mother. When he came back from the next room he brought over the chair and now he's here, sitting next to her, not saying anything, his chin on his cane and his lame leg stretched out in front of him. My grandfather's waiting. My mother, like him, is waiting too. The men have stopped smoking on the bed and they're quiet, all in a row, not looking at the coffin. They're waiting too.

If they blindfolded me, if they took me by the hand and walked me around town twenty times and brought me back to this room I'd recognize it by the smell. I'll never forget how this room smells of trash, piled-up trunks, all the same, even though I've only seen one trunk, where Abraham and I could hide and there'd still be room left over for Tobías. I know rooms by their smell.

Last year Ada sat me on her lap. I had my eyes closed and I saw her through my lashes. I saw her dark, as if she wasn't a woman but just a face that was looking at me and rocking and bleating like a sheep. I was really going to sleep when I got the smell.

There's no smell at home that I can't recognize. When they leave me alone on the veranda I close my eyes, stick out my arms, and walk. I think: *When I get the smell of camphorated rum I'll be by my grandfather's room.* I keep on walking with my eyes closed and my arms stretched out. I think: *Now I've gone past my mother's room, because it smells like new playing cards. Then it will smell of pitch and mothballs.* I keep on walking and I get the smell of new playing cards at the exact moment I hear my mother's voice singing in her room. Then I get the smell of pitch and mothballs. I think: *Now I'll keep on smelling mothballs. Then I'll turn to the left of the smell and I'll get the other smell of underwear and closed windows. I'll stop there.* Then, when I take three steps, I get the new smell and I stop, with my eyes closed and my arms outstretched, and I hear Ada's voice shouting: "Child, what are you walking with your eyes closed for?"

That night, when I began to fall asleep, I caught a smell that doesn't exist in any of the rooms in the house. It was a strong and warm smell, as if someone had been shaking a jasmine bush. I opened my eyes, sniffing the thick and heavy air. I said. "Do you smell it?" Ada was looking at me but when I spoke to her she closed her eyes and looked in the other direction. I asked her again: "Do you smell it? It's as if there were some jasmines somewhere." Then she said:

"It's the smell of the jasmines that used to be growing on the wall here nine years ago."

I sat on her lap. "But there aren't any jasmines now," I said. And she said: "Not now. But nine years ago, when you were born, there was a jasmine bush against the courtyard wall. It would be hot at night and it would smell the same as now." I leaned on her shoulder. I looked at her mouth while she spoke. "But that was before I was born," I said. And she said: "During that time there was a great winter storm and they had to clean out the garden."

The smell was still there, warm, almost touchable, leading the other smells of the night. I told Ada: "I *want* you to tell me that." And she remained silent for an instant, then looked toward the whitewashed wall with moonlight on it and said:

"When you're older you'll learn that the jasmine is a flower that *comes out*."

I didn't understand, but I felt a strange shudder, as if someone had touched me. I said: "All right," and she said: "The same thing happens with jasmines as with people who come out and wander through the night after they're dead."

I stayed there leaning on her shoulder, not saying anything. I was thinking about other things, about the chair in the kitchen where my grandfather puts his shoes on the seat to dry when it rains. I knew from then on that there's a dead man in the kitchen and every night he sits down, without taking off his hat, looking at the ashes in the cold stove. After a moment I said: "That must be like the dead man who sits in the kitchen." Ada looked at me, opened her eyes, and asked: "What dead man?" And I said to her: "The one who sits every night in the chair where my grandfather puts his shoes to dry." And she said: "There's no dead man there. The chair's next to the stove because it's no good for anything else anymore except to dry shoes on."

That was last year. Now it's different, now I've seen a corpse and all I have to do is close my eyes to keep on seeing him inside, in the darkness of my eyes. I was going to tell my mother, but she's begun to talk to my grandfather: "Do you think something might happen?" she asks. And my grandfather lifts his chin from his cane and shakes his head. "At least I'm sure that the rice will be burned and the milk spilled in lots of houses."

VI.

At first he used to sleep till seven o'clock. He would appear in the kitchen with his collarless shirt buttoned up to the neck, his wrinkled and dirty sleeves rolled up to the elbows, his filthy pants at chest level with the belt fastened outside, well below the loops. You had the feeling that his pants were about to fall down, slide off, because there was no body to hold them up. He hadn't grown thinner, but you didn't see the military and haughty look he had the first year on his face anymore; he had the dreamy and fatigued expression of a man who doesn't know what his life will be from one minute to the next and hasn't got the least interest in finding out. He would drink his black coffee a little after seven and then go back to his room, passing out his inexpressive "Good morning" along the way.

He'd been living in our house for four years and in Macondo he was looked upon as a serious professional man in spite of the fact that his brusque manner and disordered ways built up an atmosphere about him that was more like fear than respect.

He was the only doctor in town until the banana company arrived and work started on the railroad. Then empty seats began to appear in the small room. The people who visited him during the first four years of his stay in Macondo began to drift away when the company organized a clinic for its workers. He must have seen the new directions that the leaf storm was leading to, but he didn't say anything. He still opened up the street door, sitting in his leather chair all day long until several days passed without the return of a single patient. Then he threw the bolt on the door, bought a hammock, and shut himself up in the room.

During that time Meme got into the habit of bringing him breakfast, which consisted of bananas and oranges. He would eat the fruit and throw the peels into the corner, where the Indian woman would pick them up on Saturdays, when she cleaned the bedroom. But from the way he acted, anyone would have suspected that it made little difference to him whether or not she would stop cleaning some Saturday and the room would become a dungheap.

He did absolutely nothing now. He spent his time in the hammock, rocking. Through the half-open door he could be seen in the darkness and his thin and inexpressive face, his tangled hair, the sickly vitality of his hard yellow eyes gave him the unmistakable look of a man who has begun to feel defeated by circumstances.

During the first years of his stay in our house, Adelaida appeared to be indifferent or appeared to go along with me or really did agree with my decision that he should stay in the house. But when he closed his office and left his room only at mealtime, sitting at the table with the same silent and painful apathy as always, my wife broke the dikes of her tolerance. She told me: "It's heresy to keep supporting him. It's as if we were feeding the devil." And I, always inclined in his behalf out of a complex feeling of pity, amazement, and sorrow (because even though I may try to change the shape of it now, there was a great deal of sorrow in that feeling), insisted: "We have to take care of him. He's a man who doesn't have anybody in the world and he needs understanding."

Shortly afterward the railroad began to operate. Macondo was a prosperous town, full of new faces, with a movie theater and several amusement places. At that time there was work for everyone, except for him. He kept shut up, aloof, until that morning when, all of a sudden, he made an appearance in the dining room at breakfast-time and spoke spontaneously, even with enthusiasm, about the magnificent prospects for the town. That morning I heard the words for the first time. He said: "All of this will pass when we get used to the *leaf storm*."

Months later he was frequently seen going out into the street before dusk. He would sit by the barbershop until the last hours of daylight, taking part in the conversation of the groups that gathered by the door, beside the portable dressing table, beside the high stool that the barber brought out into the street so that his customers could enjoy the coolness of dusk.

The company doctors were not satisfied with depriving him of his means of life and in 1907, when there was no longer a single patient in Macondo who remembered him and when he himself had ceased expecting any, one of the banana company doctors suggested to the mayor's office that they require all professionals in town to register their degrees. He must not have felt that he was the one they had in mind when the edict appeared one Monday on the four corners of the square. It was I who spoke to him about the convenience of complying with the requirement. But he, tranquil, indifferent, limited himself to replying: "Not me, colonel. I'm not going to get involved in any of that again." I've never been able to find out whether his papers were really in order or not. I couldn't find out if he was French, as we supposed, or if he had any remembrance of a family, which he must have had but about which he never said a word. A few weeks later, when the mayor and his secretary appeared at my house to demand of him the presentation and registration of his license, he absolutely refused to leave his room. That day—after five years of living in the same house—I suddenly realized that we didn't even know his name.

One probably didn't have to be seventeen years old (as I was then) in order to observe—from the time I saw Meme all decked out in church and afterward, when I spoke to her in the shop— that the small room in our house off the street was closed up.

Later on I found out that my stepmother had padlocked it, was opposed to anyone's touching the things that were left inside: the bed that the doctor had used until he bought the hammock; the small table with medicines from which he had removed only the money accumulated during his better years (which must have been quite a bit, because he never had any expenses in the house and it was enough for Meme to open the shop with); and, in addition, in the midst of a pile of trash and old newspapers written in his language, the washstand and some useless personal items. It seemed as if all those things had been contaminated by something my stepmother considered evil, completely diabolical.

I must have noticed that the room was closed in October or November (three years after Meme and he had left the house), because early in the following year I began to dream about Martín staying in that room. I wanted to live in it after my marriage; I prowled about it; in conversation with my stepmother I even suggested that it was already time to open the padlock and lift the unbreakable quarantine imposed on one of the most intimate and friendly parts of the house. But before the time we began sewing my wedding dress, no one spoke to me directly about the doctor and even less about the small room that was still like something of his, a fragment of his personality which could not be detached from our house while anyone who might have remembered him still lived in it.

I was going to be married before the year was up. I don't know if it was the circumstances under which my life had developed during childhood and adolescence that gave me an imprecise notion of happenings and things at that time, but what was certain was that during those months when the preparations for my wedding were going forward, I still didn't know the secret of many things. A year before I married him, I would recall Martín through a vague atmosphere of unreality. Perhaps that was why I wanted him close by, in the small room, so that I could convince myself that it was a question of a concrete man and not a fiancé I had met in a dream. But I didn't feel I had the strength to speak to my stepmother about my project. The natural thing would have been to say: "I'm going to take off the padlock. I'm going to put the table next to the window and the bed against the inside wall. I'm going to put a pot of carnations on the shelf and an aloe branch over the lintel." But my cowardice, my absolute lack of decision, was joined by the foggy image of my betrothed. I remembered him as a vague, ungraspable figure whose only concrete elements seemed to be his shiny mustache, his head tilting slightly to the left, and the ever-present four-button jacket.

He had come to our house toward the end of July. He spent the day with us and chatted with my father in the office, going over some mysterious business that I was never able to find out about. In the afternoon Martín and I would go to the plantations with my stepmother. But when I looked at him on the way back in the mellow light of sunset, when he was closer to me, walking alongside my shoulder, then he became even more abstract and unreal. I knew that I would never be capable of imagining him as human or of finding in him the solidity that was indispensable if his memory was to give me courage, strengthen me at the moment of saying: "I'm going to fix the room up for Martín."

Even the idea that I was going to marry him seemed odd to me a year before the wedding. I had met him in February, during the wake for the Paloquemado child. Several of us girls were singing and clapping, trying to use up every drop of the only fun allowed us. There was a movie theater in Macondo, there was a public phonograph, and other places for amusement existed, but my father and stepmother were opposed to girls my age making use of them. "They're amusements from out of the leaf storm," they said.

Noontime was hot in February. My stepmother and I were sitting on the veranda, backstitching some white cloth while my father took his siesta. We sewed until he went by, dragging along in his clogs, to soak his head in the washbasin. But February was cool and deep at night and in the whole town one could hear the voices of women singing at wakes for children.

The night we went to the Paloquemado child's wake Meme Orozco's voice was probably louder than ever. She was thin, graceless, and stiff, like a broom, but she knew how to make her voice carry better than anyone. And in the first pause Genoveva García said: "There's a stranger sitting outside." I think that all of us stopped singing except Remedios Orozco. "Just think, he's wearing a jacket," Genoveva García said. "He's been talking all night and the others are listening to him without saying a peep. He's wearing a four-button jacket and when he crosses his legs you can see his socks and garters and his shoes have laces." Meme Orozco was still singing when we clapped our hands and said: "Let's marry him."

Afterward, when I thought about it at home, I couldn't find any correspondence between those words and reality. I remembered them as if they had been spoken by a group of imaginary women clapping hands and singing in a house where an unreal child had died. Other women were smoking next to us. They were serious, vigilant, stretching out their long buzzard necks toward us. In the back, against the coolness of the doorstep, another woman, bundled up to her head in a wide black cloth, was waiting for the coffee to boil. Suddenly a male voice joined ours. At first it was disconcerted and directionless, but then it was vibrant and metallic, as if the man were singing in church. Veva García nudged me in the ribs. Then I raised my eyes and saw him for the first time. He was young and neat, with a hard collar and a jacket with all four buttons closed. And he was looking at me.

I heard about his return in December and I thought that no place would be more appropriate for him than the small locked room. But I hadn't thought of it yet. I said to myself: "Martín, Martín, Martín." And the name, examined, savored, broken down into its essential parts, lost all of its meaning for me.

When we came out of the wake he put an empty cup in front of me. He said: "I read your fortune in the coffee." I was going to the door with the other girls and I heard his voice, deep, convincing, gentle: "Count seven stars and you'll dream about me." When we passed by the door we saw the Paloquemado child in his small coffin, his face powdered, a rose in his mouth, and his eyes held open with toothpicks. February was sending us warm gusts of death, and the breath of the jasmines and the violets toasted by the heat floated in the room. But in that silence of a dead person, the other voice was constant and different: "Remember. Only seven stars."

He came to our house in July. He liked to lean back against the flowerpots along the railing. He said: "Remember, I never looked into your eyes. That's the secret of a man who's begun to sense the fear of falling in love." And it was true, I couldn't remember his eyes. In July I probably couldn't have said what color the eyes of the man I was going to marry in December were. Still, six months earlier, February was only a deep silence at noontime, a pair of congorocho worms, male and female, coiled on the bathroom floor, the Tuesday beggar woman asking for a branch of lemon balm, and he, leaning back, smiling, his jacket buttoned all the way up, saying: "I'm going to make you think about me every minute of the day. I put a picture of you behind the door and I stuck two pins in your eyes." And Genoveva García, dying with laughter: "That's the kind of nonsense men pick up from the Guajiro Indians."

Toward the end of March he would be going through the house. He would spend long hours in the office with my father, convincing him of the importance of something I could never decipher. Eleven years have passed now since my marriage; nine since the time I watched him say good-bye from the window of the train, making me promise I would take good care of the child until he came back for us. Those nine years would pass with no one's hearing a word from him, and my father, who had helped him get ready for that endless trip, never said another word about his return. But not even during the two years that our marriage lasted was he more concrete and touchable than he was at the wake for the Paloquemado child or on that Sunday in March when I saw him for the second time as Veva García and I were coming home from church. He was standing in the doorway of the hotel, alone, his hands in the side pockets of his four-button jacket. He said: "Now you're going to think about me for the rest of your life because the pins have fallen out of the picture." He said it in such a soft and tense voice that it sounded like the truth. But even that truth was strange and different. Genoveva insisted: "That's silly Guajiro stuff." Three months later she ran away with the head of a company of puppeteers, but she still seemed scrupulous and serious on that Sunday. Martín said: "It's nice to know that someone will remember me in Macondo." And Genoveva García, looking at him with a face that showed exasperation, said:

"*Airyfay!* That four-button coat's going to rot with you inside of it."

VII.

Even though he hoped it would be the opposite, he was a strange person in town, apathetic in spite of his obvious efforts to seem sociable and cordial. He lived among the people of Macondo, but at a distance from them because of the memory of a past against which any attempt at rectification seemed useless. He was looked on with curiosity, like a gloomy animal who had spent a long time in the shadows and was reappearing, conducting himself in a way that the town could only consider as superimposed and therefore suspect.

He would come back from the barbershop at nightfall and shut himself up in his room. For some time he had given up his evening meal and at first the impression at home was that he was coming back fatigued and going directly to his hammock to sleep until the following day. But only a short time passed before I began to realize that something extraordinary was happening to him at night. He could be heard moving about in his room with a tormented and maddening insistence, as if on those nights he was receiving the ghost of the man he had been until then, and both of them, the past man and the present one, were locked in a silent struggle in which the past one was defending his wrathful solitude, his invulnerable standoffish way, his intransigent manners; and the present one his terrible and unchangeable will to free himself from his own previous man. I could hear him pacing about the room until dawn, until the time his own fatigue had exhausted the strength of his invisible adversary.

I was the only one who noticed the true measure of his change, from the time he stopped wearing leggings and began to take a bath every day and perfume his clothing with scented water. And a few months later his transformation had reached the level where my feelings toward him stopped being a simple understanding tolerance and changed into compassion. It was not his new look on the street that moved me. It was thinking of him shut up in his room at night, scraping the mud off his boots, wetting a rag in the washstand, spreading polish on the shoes that had deteriorated through many years of continuous use. It moved me to think of the brush and box of shoe polish kept under the mattress, hidden from the eyes of the world as if they were the elements of a secret and shameful vice contracted at an age when the majority of men were becoming serene and methodical. For all practical purposes, he was going through a tardy and sterile adolescence and, like an adolescent, he took great care in his dress, smoothing out his clothing every night with the edge of his hand, coldly, and he was not young enough to have a friend to whom he could communicate his illusions or his disillusions.

The town must have noticed his change too, for a short time

later it began to be said about that he was in love with the barber's daughter. I don't know whether there was any basis for that, but what was certain was that the bit of gossip made me realize his tremendous sexual loneliness, the biological fury that must have tormented him in those years of filth and abandonment.

Every afternoon he could be seen passing by on his way to the barbershop, more and more fastidious in his dress. A shirt with an artificial collar, gold cuff links, and his pants clean and pressed, except that he still wore his belt outside the loops. He looked like an afflicted suitor, enveloped in the aura of cheap lotions; the eternal frustrated suitor, the sunset lover who would always lack the bouquet of flowers on the first visit.

That was how he was during the first months of 1909, with still no basis for the gossip in town except for the fact that he would be seen sitting in the barbershop every afternoon chatting with strangers, but with no one's having been able to be sure that he'd ever seen him a single time with the barber's daughter. I discovered the cruelty of that gossip. Everyone in town knew that the barber's daughter would always be an old maid after going through a year of suffering, as she was pursued by a *spirit*, an invisible lover who spread dirt on her food and muddied the water in the pitcher and fogged the mirrors in the barbershop and beat her until her face was green and disfigured. The efforts of the Pup, with a stroke of his stole, the complex therapy of holy water, sacred relics, and psalms administered with dramatic solicitude, were useless. As an extreme measure, the barber's wife locked her bewitched daughter up in her room, strewed rice about the living room, and turned her over to the invisible lover in a solitary and dead honeymoon, after which even the men of Macondo said that the barber's daughter had conceived.

Not even a year had passed when people stopped waiting for the monstrous event of her giving birth and public curiosity turned to the idea that the doctor was in love with the barber's daughter, in spite of the fact that everyone was convinced that the bewitched girl would lock herself up in her room and crumble to pieces in life long before any possible suitors would be transformed into marriageable men.

That was why I knew that rather than a supposition with some basis, it was a piece of cruel gossip, maliciously premeditated. Toward the end of 1909 he was still going to the barbershop and people were talking, organizing the wedding, with no one able to say that the girl had ever come out when he was present or that they had ever had a chance to speak to each other.

One September that was as broiling and as dead as this one, thirteen years ago, my stepmother began sewing on my wedding dress. Every afternoon while my father took his siesta, we would sit down to sew beside the flowerpots on the railing, next to the burning stove that was the rosemary plant. September has been like this all of my life, since thirteen years ago and much longer. As my wedding was to take place in a private ceremony (because my father had decided on it), we sewed slowly, with the minute care of a person who is in no hurry and has found the best measure of her time in her imperceptible work. We would talk during those times. I was still thinking about the street room, gathering up the courage to tell my stepmother that it was the best place to put up Martín. And that afternoon I told her.

My stepmother was sewing the long train of lace and it seemed in the blinding light of that intolerably clear and sound-filled September that she was submerged up to her shoulders in a cloud of that very September. "No," my stepmother said. And then, going back to her work, feeling eight years of bitter memories passing in front of her: "May God never permit anyone to enter that room again."

Martín had returned in July, but he didn't stay at our house. He liked to lean against the railing and stay there looking in the opposite direction. It pleased him to say: "I'd like to spend the rest of my life in Macondo." In the afternoon we'd go out to the plantations with my stepmother. We'd come back at dinnertime, before the lights in town went on. Then he'd tell me: "Even if it hadn't been for you, I'd like to live in Macondo in any case." And that too, from the way he said it, seemed to be the truth.

Around that time it had been four years since the doctor had left our house. And it was precisely on the afternoon we had begun work on the wedding dress—that suffocating afternoon when I told her about the room for Martín—that my stepmother spoke to me for the first time about his strange ways.

"Five years ago," she said, "he was still there, shut up like an animal. Because he wasn't only that, an animal, but something else: an animal who ate grass, a ruminant like any ox in a yoke. If he'd married the barber's daughter, that little faker who made the whole town believe the great lie that she'd conceived after a murky honeymoon with the spirits, maybe none of this would have happened. But he stopped going to the barbershop all of a sudden and he even showed a last-minute change that was only a new chapter as he methodically went through with his frightful plan. Only your father could have thought that after all that a man of such base habits should still stay in our house, living like an animal, scandalizing the town, giving people cause to talk about us as people who were always defying morals and good habits. His plans would end up with Meme's leaving. But not even then did your father recognize the alarming proportions of his mistake."

"I never heard any of that," I said. The locusts had set up a sawmill in the courtyard. My stepmother was speaking, still sewing without lifting her eyes from the tambour where she was stitching symbols, embroidering white labyrinths. She said: "That night we were sitting at the table (all except him, because ever since the afternoon he came back from the barbershop for the last time he wouldn't take his evening meal) when Meme came to

serve us. She was different. 'What's the matter, Meme?' I asked
her. 'Nothing, ma'am. Why?' But we could see that she wasn't
right because she hesitated next to the lamp and she had a sickly
look all over her. 'Good heavens, Meme, you're not well,' I said.
But she held herself up as best she could until she turned toward
the kitchen with the tray. Then your father, who was watching
all the time, said to her: 'If you don't feel well, go to bed.' But
she didn't say anything. She went out with the tray, her back
to us, until we heard the noise of the dishes as they broke to
pieces. Meme was on the veranda, holding herself up against the
wall by her fingernails. That was when your father went to get
that one in the bedroom to have a look at Meme.

"During the eight years he spent in our house," my stepmother
said, "we'd never asked for his services for anything serious. We
women went to Meme's room, rubbed her with alcohol, and
waited for your father to come back. But they didn't come, Isabel.
He didn't come to look at Meme in spite of the fact that the man
who had fed him for eight years, had given him lodging and had
his clothes washed, had gone to get him in person. Every time I
remember him I think that his coming here was God's punishment. I think that all that grass we gave him for eight years,
all the care, all the solicitude was a test of God's, teaching us a
lesson in prudence and mistrust of the world. It was as if we'd
taken eight years of hospitality, food, clean clothes, and thrown
it all to the hogs. Meme was dying (at least we thought she was)
and he, right there, was still shut up, refusing to go through with
what was no longer a work of charity but one of decency, of
thanks, of simple consideration for those who were taking care of
him.

"Only at midnight did your father come back. He said weakly:
'Give her some alcohol rubs, but no physics.' And I felt as if I'd
been slapped. Meme had responded to our rubbing. Infuriated, I
shouted: 'Yes! Alcohol, that's it! We've already rubbed her and
she's better! But in order to do that we didn't have to live eight

years sponging off people!' And your father, still condescending, still with that conciliatory nonsense: 'It's nothing serious. You'll realize that someday.' As if that other one were some sort of soothsayer."

That afternoon, because of the vehemence of her voice, the exaltation of her words, it seemed as if my stepmother were seeing again what happened on that remote night when the doctor refused to attend to Meme. The rosemary bush seemed suffocated by the blinding clarity of September, by the drowsiness of the locusts, by the heavy breathing of the men trying to take down a door in the neighborhood.

"But one of those Sundays Meme went to mass all decked out like a lady of quality," she said. "I can remember it as if it were today. She had a parasol with changing colors.

"Meme. Meme. That was God's punishment too. We'd taken her from where her parents were starving her to death, we took care of her, gave her a roof over her head, food, and a name, but the hand of Providence intervened there too. When I saw her at the door the next day, waiting for one of the Indians to carry her trunk out for her, even I didn't know where she was going. She was changed and serious, right over there (I can see her now), standing beside the trunk, talking to your father. Everything had been done without consulting me, Chabela; as if I were a painted puppet on the wall. Before I could ask what was going on, why strange things were happening in my own house without my knowing about them, your father came to tell me: 'You've nothing to ask Meme. She's leaving, but maybe she'll come back after a while.' I asked him where she was going and he didn't answer me. He was dragging along in his clogs as if I weren't his wife but some painted puppet on the wall.

"Only two days later," she said, "did I find out that the other one had left at dawn without the decency of saying good-bye. He'd come here as if the place belonged to him and eight years later he left as if he were leaving his own house, without saying good-bye, without saying anything. Just the way a thief would have done. I thought your father had sent him away for not attending to Meme, but when I asked him that or the same day, he limited himself to answering: 'You and I have to have a long talk about that.' And four years have passed without his ever bringing up the subject with me again.

"Only with your father and in a house as disordered as this one, where everybody does whatever he wants to, could such a thing have happened. In Macondo they weren't talking about anything else and I still didn't know that Meme had appeared in church all decked out, like a nobody raised to the status of a lady, and that your father had had the nerve to lead her across the square by the arm. That was when I found out that she wasn't as far away as I'd thought, but was living in the house on the corner with the doctor. They'd gone to live together like two pigs, not even going through the door of the church even though she'd been baptized. One day I told your father: 'God will punish that bit of heresy too.' And he didn't say anything. He was still the same tranquil man he always was, even after having been the patron of public concubinage and scandal.

"And yet I'm pleased now that things turned out that way, just so that the doctor left our house. If that hadn't happened, he'd still be in the little room. But when I found out that he'd left it and that he was taking his trash to the corner along with that trunk that wouldn't fit through the street door, I felt more peaceful. That was my victory, postponed for eight years.

"Two weeks later Meme opened the store, and she even had a sewing machine. She'd bought a new Domestic with the money she put away in this house. I considered that an affront and that's what I told your father. But even though he didn't answer my protests, you could see that instead of being sorry, he was satisfied with his work, as if he'd saved his soul by going against what was proper and honorable for this house, with his proverbial tolerance, his understanding, his liberality. And even a little empty-headedness. I said to him: 'You've thrown the best part of your beliefs to the swine.' And he, as always:

" 'You'll understand that too someday.' "

VIII.

December arrived like an unexpected spring, as a book once described it. And Martín arrived along with it. He appeared at the house after lunch, with a collapsible suitcase, still wearing the four-button jacket, clean and freshly pressed now. He said nothing to me but went directly to my father's office to talk to him. The date for the wedding had been set since July. But two days after Martín's arrival in December, my father called my stepmother to the office to tell her that the wedding would take place on Monday. It was Saturday.

My dress was finished. Martín had been to the house every day. He spoke to my father and the latter would give us his impressions at mealtime. I didn't know my fiancé. I hadn't been alone with him at any time. Still, Martín seemed to be linked to my father by a deep and solid friendship, and my father spoke of him as if it were he and not I who was going to marry Martín.

I felt no emotion over the closeness of the wedding date. I was still wrapped up in that gray cloud which Martín came through, stiff and abstract, moving his arms as he spoke, closing and opening his four-button jacket. He had lunch with us on Sunday. My stepmother assigned the places at the table in such a way that Martín was next to my father, separated from me by three places. During lunch my stepmother and I said very little. My father and Martín talked about their business matter; and I, sitting three places away, looked at the man who a year later would be the father of my son and to whom I was not even joined by a superficial friendship.

On Sunday night I tried on the wedding dress in my stepmother's bedroom. I looked pale and clean in the mirror, wrapped in that cloud of powdery froth that reminded me of my mother's ghost. I said to myself in front of the mirror: "That's me. Isabel. I'm dressed as a bride who's going to be married tomorrow morning." And I didn't recognize myself; I felt weighted down with the memory of my dead mother. Meme had spoken to me about her on this same corner a few days before. She told me that after I was born my mother was dressed in her bridal clothes and placed in a coffin. And now, looking at myself in the mirror, I saw my mother's bones covered by the mold of the tomb in a pile of crumpled gauze and compact yellow dust. I was outside the mirror. Inside was my mother, alive again, looking at me, stretching her arms out from her frozen space, trying to touch the death that was held together by the first pins of my bridal veil. And in back, in the center of the bedroom, my father, serious, perplexed: "She looks just like her now in that dress."

That night I received my first, last, and only love letter. A message from Martín written in pencil on the back of a movie program. It said: *Since it will be impossible for me to get there on time tonight, I'll go to confession in the morning. Tell the colonel that the thing we were talking about is almost set and that's why I can't come now. Are you frightened?* M. With the flat, floury taste of that letter in my mouth I went to my bedroom, and my palate was still bitter when I woke up a few hours later as my stepmother shook me.

Actually, many hours passed before I woke up completely. In the wedding dress I felt again as if I were in some cool and damp dawn that smelled of musk. My mouth felt dry, as when a person is starting out on a trip and the saliva refuses to wet the bread. The bridal party had been in the living room since four o'clock. I knew them all but now they looked transformed and new, the men dressed in tweeds and the women with their hats on, talking, filling the house with the dense and enervating vapor of their words.

The church was empty. A few women turned around to look at me as I went down the center aisle like a consecrated youth on his way to the sacrificial stone. The Pup, thin and serious, the only person with a look of reality in that turbulent and silent nightmare, came down the altar steps and gave me to Martín with four movements of his emaciated hands. Martín was beside me, tranquil and smiling, the way I'd seen him at the wake of the Paloquemado child, but wearing a short collar now, as if to show me that even on his wedding day he'd taken pains to be still more abstract than he already was on ordinary days.

That morning, back at the house, after the wedding party had eaten breakfast and contributed the standard phrases, my husband went out and didn't come back until siesta time. My father and stepmother didn't seem to notice my situation. They let the day pass without changing the order of things, so that nothing would make the extraordinary breath of that Monday felt. I took my wedding gown apart, made a bundle of it, and put it in the bottom of the wardrobe, remembering my mother, thinking: *At least these rags can be my shroud.*

The unreal groom returned at two in the afternoon and said that he had had lunch. Then it seemed to me as I watched him come with his short hair that December was no longer a blue month. Martín sat down beside me and we remained there for a moment without speaking. For the first time since I had been born I was afraid for night to begin. I must have shown it in some expression, because all of a sudden Martín seemed to come to life; he leaned over my shoulder and asked: "What are you thinking about?" I felt something twisting in my heart: the stranger had begun to address me in the familiar form. I looked up toward where December was a gigantic shining ball, a luminous glass month; I said: "I was thinking that all we need now is for it to start raining."

*   *   *

The last night we spoke on the veranda it was hotter than usual. A few days later he would return for good from the barbershop and shut himself up in his room. But on that last night on the veranda, one of the hottest and heaviest I can remember, he seemed understanding as on few occasions. The only thing that seemed alive in the midst of that immense oven was the dull reverberation of the crickets, aroused by the thirst of nature, and the tiny, insignificant, and yet measureless activity of the rosemary and the nard, burning in the middle of the deserted hour. Both of us remained silent for a moment, exuding that thick and viscous substance that isn't sweat but the loose drivel of decomposing living matter. Sometimes he would look at the stars, in a sky desolate because of the summer splendor; then he would remain silent, as if completely given over to the passage of that night, which was monstrously alive. That was how we were, pensive, face to face, he in his leather chair, I in the rocker. Suddenly, with the passage of a white wing, I saw him tilt his sad and lonely head over his left shoulder. I thought of his life, his solitude, his frightful spiritual disturbances. I thought of the tormented indifference with which he watched the spectacle of life. Previously I had felt drawn to him out of complex feelings, sometimes contradictory and as variable as his personality. But at that moment there wasn't the slightest doubt in me that I'd begun to love him deeply. I thought that inside of myself I'd uncovered the mysterious force that from the first moment had led me to shelter him, and I felt the pain of his dark and stifling room like an open wound. I saw him as somber and defeated, crushed by circumstances. And suddenly, with a new look from his hard and penetrating yellow eyes, I felt the certainty that the secret of his labyrinthine solitude had been revealed to me by the tense pulsation of the night. Before I even had time to think why I was doing it, I asked him:

"Tell me something, doctor. Do you believe in God?"

He looked at me. His hair fell over his forehead and a kind of inner suffocation burned all through him, but his face still showed no shadow of emotion or upset. Having completely recovered his parsimonious ruminant voice, he said:

"It's the first time anyone ever asked me that question."

"What about you, doctor, have you ever asked it?"

He seemed neither indifferent nor concerned. He only seemed interested in my person. Not even in my question and least of all in its intent.

"That's hard to say," he said.

"But doesn't a night like this make you afraid? Don't you get the feeling that there's a man bigger than all of us walking through the plantations while nothing moves and everything seems perplexed at the passage of that man?"

He was silent then. The crickets filled the surrounding space, beyond the warm smell which was alive and almost human as it rose up from the jasmine bush I had planted in memory of my first wife. A man without dimensions was walking alone through the night.

"I really don't think any of that bothers me, colonel." And now he seemed perplexed, he too, like things, like the rosemary and the nard in their burning place. "What bothers me," he said, and he kept on looking into my eyes, directly, sternly, "what bothers me is that there's a person like you capable of saying with such certainty that he's aware of that man walking in the night."

"We try to save our souls, doctor. That's the difference."

And then I went beyond what I had proposed. I said: "You don't hear him because you're an atheist."

And he, serene, unperturbed:

"Believe me, colonel, I'm not an atheist. I get just as upset thinking that God exists as thinking that he doesn't. That's why I'd rather not think about it."

I don't know why, but I had the feeling that that was exactly what he was going to answer. *He's a man disturbed by God*, I thought, listening to what he'd just told me spontaneously, with clarity, precision, as if he'd read it in a book. I was still intoxicated with the drowsiness of the night. I felt that I was in the heart of an immense gallery of prophetic images.

Over there on the other side of the railing was the small garden where Adelaida and my daughter had planted things. That was why the rosemary was burning, because every morning they strengthened it with their attention so that on nights like that its burning vapor would pass through the house and make sleep more restful. The jasmine gave off its insistent breath and we received it because it was the same age as Isabel, because in a certain way that smell was a prolongation of her mother. The crickets were in the courtyard, among the bushes, because we'd neglected to clean out the weeds when it had stopped raining. The only thing incredible, miraculous, was that he was there, with his enormous cheap handkerchief, drying his forehead, which glowed with perspiration.

Then after another pause, he said:

"I'd like to know why you asked me that, colonel."

"It just came to me all of a sudden," I said. "Maybe after seven years I wanted to know what a man like you thinks about."

I was mopping my brow too. I said:

"Or maybe I'm worried about your solitude." I waited for an answer that didn't come. I saw him across from me, still sad and alone. I thought about Macondo, the madness of its people, burning banknotes at parties; about the leaf storm that had no direction and was above everything, wallowing in its slough of instinct and dissipation where it had found the taste it wanted. I thought about his life before the leaf storm had struck. And his life afterward, his cheap perfume, his polished old shoes, the gossip that followed him like a shadow that he himself ignored. I said:

"Doctor, have you ever thought of taking a wife?"

And before I could finish asking the question, he was giving an answer, starting off on one of his usual long meanderings:

"You love your daughter very much, don't you, colonel?"

67

I answered that it was natural. He went on speaking:

"All right. But you're different. Nobody likes to drive his own nails more than you. I've seen you putting hinges on a door when there are several men working for you who could have done it. You like that. I think that your happiness is to walk about the house with a toolbox looking for something to fix. You're even capable of thanking a person for having broken a hinge, colonel. You thank him because in that way he's giving you a chance to be happy."

"It's a habit," I told him, not knowing what direction he was taking. "They say my mother was the same way."

He'd reacted. His attitude was peaceful but ironclad.

"Fine," he said. "It's a good habit. Besides, it's the cheapest kind of happiness I know. That's why you have a house like this and raised your daughter the way you have. I say that it must be good to have a daughter like yours."

I still didn't know what he was getting at in his long, roundabout way. But even though I didn't know, I asked:

"What about you, doctor, haven't you ever thought about how nice it would be to have a daughter?"

"Not I, colonel," he said. And he smiled, but then he immediately became serious again. "My children wouldn't be like yours."

Then I didn't have the slightest trace of doubt: he was talking seriously and that seriousness, that situation, seemed frightful to me. I was thinking: *He's more to be pitied for that than for anything else.* He needed protection, I thought.

"Have you heard of the Pup?" I asked him.

He said no. I told him: "The Pup is the parish priest, but more than that he's a friend to everybody. You should get to know him."

"Oh, yes, yes," he said. "He has children *too*, right?"

"That's not what interests me right now," I said. "People invent bits of gossip about the Pup because they have a lot of love for him. But you have a point there, doctor. The Pup is a long way from being a prayermonger, sanctimonious, as we say. He's a whole man who fulfills his duties as a man."

Now he was listening with attention. He was silent, concentrating, his hard yellow eyes fastened on mine. He said: "That's good, right?"

"I think the Pup will be made a saint," I said. And I was sincere in that too. "We've never seen anything like him in Macondo. At first they didn't trust him because he comes from here, because the older people remembered him from when he used to go out hunting birds like all the boys. He fought in the war, he was a colonel, and that was a problem. You know how people are, no respect for veterans, the same as with priests. Besides, we weren't used to having someone read to us from the Bristol Almanac instead of the Gospels."

He smiled. That must have sounded as odd to him as it had to us during the first days. He said: "That's strange, isn't it?"

"That's the way the Pup is. He'd rather show people by means of atmospheric phenomena. He's got a preoccupation with storms that's almost theological. He talks about them every Sunday. And that's why his sermons aren't based on the Gospels but on the atmospheric predictions in the Bristol Almanac."

He was smiling now and listening with a lively and pleased expression. I felt enthusiastic too. I said: "There's still something else of interest for you, doctor. Do you know how long the Pup has been in Macondo?"

He said no.

"It so happens that he arrived the same day as you," I said. "And what's even stranger still, if you had an older brother, I'm sure that he'd be just like the Pup. Physically, of course."

He didn't seem to be thinking about anything else now. From his seriousness, from his concentrated and steady attention, I sensed that I had come to the moment to tell him what I wanted to propose:

"Well, then, doctor," I said. "Pay a call on the Pup and you'll find out that things aren't the way you see them."

And he said yes, he'd visit the Pup.

IX.

Coldly, silently, progressively, the padlock gathers rust. Adelaida put it on the room when she found out that the doctor had gone to live with Meme. My wife considered that move as a victory for her, the culminaton of a systematic, tenacious piece of work she had started the first moment I decided that he would live with us. Seventeen years later the padlock is still guarding the room.

If there was something in my attitude, unchanged for eight years, that may have seemed unworthy in the eyes of men or ungrateful in those of God, my punishment has come about a long time before my death. Perhaps it was meant for me to expiate in life for what I had considered a human obligation, a Christian duty. Because the rust on the lock had not begun to accumulate when Martín was in my house with a briefcase full of projects, the authenticity of which I've never been able to find out, and the firm desirè to marry my daughter. He came to my house in a four-button jacket, exuding youth and dynamism from all his pores, enveloped in a luminous air of pleasantness. He married Isabel in December eleven years ago. Nine have passed since he went off with the briefcase full of notes signed by me and with the promise to return as soon as the deal he was working on and for which he had my financial backing came through. Nine years have gone by but I have no right to think he was a swindler because of that. I have no right to think his marriage was only a pretext to convince me of his good faith.

But eight years of experience have been of some use. Martín could have occupied the small room. Adelaida was against it. Her opposition was adamant, decisive and irrevocable. I knew that my wife wouldn't have been bothered in the least to fix up the stable as a bridal chamber rather than let the newlyweds occupy the small room. I accepted her point of view without hesitation. That was my recognition of her victory, one postponed for eight years. If both of us were mistaken in trusting Martín, it was a mistake that was shared. There was neither victory nor defeat for either one of us. Still, what came later was too much for our efforts, it was like the atmospheric phenoména the almanac foretells, ones that must come no matter what.

When I told Meme to leave our house, to follow the direction she thought best for her life, and afterward, even though Adelaida threw my weaknesses and lack of strength up to me, I was able to rebel, to impose my will on everything (that's what I've always done) and arrange things my way. But something told me that I was powerless before the course that events were taking. It wasn't I who arranged things in my own home, but some other mysterious force, one which decided the course of our existence and of which we were nothing but docile and insignificant instruments. Everything seemed to obey the natural and linked fulfillment of a prophecy.

Since Meme was able to open the shop (underneath it all everybody must have known that a hard-working woman who becomes the mistress of a country doctor overnight will sooner or later end up as a shopkeeper), I realized that in our house he'd accumulated a larger sum of money than one might have imagined, and that he'd kept it in his cabinet, uncounted bills and coins which he tossed into the drawer during the time he saw patients.

When Meme opened the shop it was supposed that he was here, in back of the store, shut up because of God knows what bestial and implacable prophecies. It was known that he wouldn't eat any food from outside, that he'd planted a garden and that during the first months Meme would buy a piece of meat for herself, but that a year later she'd stopped doing that, perhaps because direct contact with the man had made a vegetarian of her. Then the two of them shut themselves up until the time the authorities broke down the door, searched the house, and dug up the garden in an attempt to find Meme's body.

People imagined him there, shut in, rocking in his old and tattered hammock. But I knew, even in those months during which his return to the world of the living was not expected, that his impenitent enclosure, his muted battle against the threat of God, would reach its culmination much sooner than his death. I knew that sooner or later he would come out because there isn't a man alive who can live a half-life, locked up, far away from God, without coming out all of a sudden to render to the first man he meets on the corner the accounts that stocks and pillory, the martyrdom of fire and water, the torture of the rack and the screw, wood and hot iron on his eyes, the eternal salt on his tongue, the torture horse, lashes, the grate, and love could not have made him render to his inquisitors. And that time would come for him a few years before his death.

I knew that truth from before, from the last night we talked on the veranda, and afterward, when I went to get him in the little room to have a look at Meme. Could I have opposed his desire to live with her as man and wife? I might have been able before. Not now, because another chapter of fate had begun to be fulfilled three months before that.

He wasn't in his hammock that night. He'd lain down on his back on the cot and had his head back, his eyes fixed on the spot on the ceiling where the light from the candle must have been most intense. There was an electric light in the room but he never used it. He preferred to lie in the shadows, his eyes fixed on the darkness. He didn't move when I went into the room, but I noticed that the moment I crossed the threshold he felt that he wasn't alone. Then I said: "If it's not too much trouble, doctor, it seems that the Indian girl isn't feeling well." He sat up on the bed. A moment before he'd felt that he wasn't alone in the room.

Now he knew that I was the one who was there. Without doubt they were two completely different feelings, because he underwent an immediate change, he smoothed his hair and remained sitting on the edge of the bed, waiting.

"It's Adelaida, doctor. She wants you to come look at Meme," I said.

And he, sitting there, gave me the impact of an answer with his parsimonious ruminant voice:

"It won't be necessary. The fact is she's pregnant."

Then he leaned forward, seemed to be examining my face, and said: "Meme's been sleeping with me for years."

I must confess that I was surprised. I didn't feel any upset, perplexity, or anger. I didn't feel anything. Perhaps his confession was too serious to my way of seeing things and was out of the normal course of my comprehension. I remained impassive and I didn't even know why. I was motionless, standing, immutable, as cold as he, like his parsimonious ruminant voice. Then, after a long silence during which he still sat on the cot, not moving, as if waiting for me to take the first step, I understood what he had just told me in all of its intensity. But then it was too late for me to get upset.

"As long as you're aware of the situation, doctor." That was all I could say. He said:

"One takes his precautions, colonel. When a person takes a risk he knows that he's taking it. If something goes wrong it's because there was something unforeseen, out of a person's reach."

I knew that kind of evasion. As always, I didn't know where he was leading. I brought over a chair and sat down opposite him. Then he left the cot, fastened the buckle of his belt, and pulled up his pants and adjusted them. He kept on talking from the other end of the room. He said:

"Just as sure as the fact that I took my precautions is the fact that this is the second time she's got pregnant. The first time was a year and a half ago and you people didn't notice anything."

He went on talking without emotion, going back to the cot. In the darkness I heard his slow, firm steps against the tiles. He said:

"But she was ready for anything then. Not now. Two months ago she told me she was pregnant again and I told her what I had the first time: 'Come by tonight and be ready for the same thing.' She told me not that day, the next day. When I went to have my coffee in the kitchen I told her that I was waiting for her, but she said that she'd never come back."

He'd come over by the cot, but he didn't sit down. He turned his back on me again and began to walk around the room once more. I heard him speaking. I heard the flow of his voice, back and forth, as if he were rocking in the hammock. He was telling things calmly, but with assurance. I knew that it would have been useless to try to interrupt him. All I could do was listen to him. And he kept on talking:

"Still, she did come two days later. I had everything ready. I told her to sit down there and I went to my table for the glass. Then, when I told her to drink it, I realized that this time she wouldn't. She looked at me without smiling and said with a touch of cruelty: 'I'm not going to get rid of this one, doctor. This one I'm going to have so I can raise it.' "

I felt exasperated by his calmness. I told him: "That doesn't justify anything, doctor. What you've done is something that's twice unworthy: first, because of your relations inside my house, and then because of the abortion."

"But you can see that I did everything I could, colonel. It was all I could do. Afterward, when I saw there was no way out, I got ready to talk to you. I was going to do it one of these days."

"I imagine you know that there is a way out of this kind of situation if you really want to erase the insult. You know the principles of those of us who live in this house," I said.

And he said:

"I don't want to cause you any trouble, colonel. Believe me. What I was going to tell you is this: I'll take the Indian woman and go live in the empty house on the corner."

"Living together openly, doctor?" I asked him. "Do you know what that means for us?"

Then he went back to the cot. He sat down, leaned forward, and spoke with his elbows on his legs. His accent became different. At first it had been cold. Now it began to be cruel and challenging. He said:

"I'm proposing the only solution that won't cause you any distress, colonel. The other thing would be to say that the child isn't mine."

"Meme would say it was," I said. I was beginning to feel indignant. His way of expressing himself was too challenging and aggressive now and I couldn't accept it calmly.

But he, hard, implacable, said:

"You have to believe me absolutely when I say that Meme won't say it is. It's because I'm sure of that that I say I'll take her to the corner, only so I can avoid distress for you. That's the only reason, colonel."

He was so sure that Meme would not attribute the paternity of her child to him that now I did feel upset. Something was making me think that his strength was rooted much deeper than his words. I said:

"We trust Meme as we would our own daughter, doctor. In this case she'd be on our side."

"If you knew what I know, you wouldn't talk that way, colonel. Pardon me for saying it this way, but if you compare that Indian girl to your daughter, you're insulting your daughter."

"You have no reason to say that," I said.

And he answered, still with that bitter hardness in his voice: "I do. And when I tell you that she can't say that I'm the father of her child, I also have reasons for it."

75

He threw his head back. He sighed deeply and said:

"If you took time to spy on Meme when she goes out at night, you wouldn't even demand that I take her away with me. In this case I'm the one who runs the risk, colonel. I'm taking on a dead man to avoid your having any distress."

Then I understood that he wouldn't even go through the doors of the church with Meme. But what was serious was that after his final words I wouldn't have dared go through with what could have been a tremendous burden on my conscience later on. There were several cards in my favor. But the single one he held would have been enough for him to win a bet against my conscience.

"All right, doctor," I said. "This very night I'll make arrangements to have the house on the corner fixed up. But in any case, I want you to be aware of the fact that I'm throwing you out of my house. You're not leaving of your own free will. Colonel Aureliano Buendía would have made you pay dearly for the way you returned his trust."

And when I thought I'd roused up his instincts and was waiting for him to unleash his dark, primal forces, he threw the whole weight of his dignity on me.

"You're a decent man, colonel," he said. "Everybody knows that, and I've lived in this house long enough for you not to have to remind me of it."

When he stood up he didn't seem victorious. He only seemed satisfied at having been able to repay our attentions of eight years. I was the one who felt upset, the one at fault. That night, seeing the germs of death that were becoming progressively more visible in his hard yellow eyes, I understood that my attitude was selfish and that because of that one single stain on my conscience it would be quite right for me to suffer a tremendous expiation for the rest of my life. He, on the other hand, was at peace with himself. He said:

"As for Meme, have them rub her with alcohol. But they shouldn't give her any physics."

X.

My grandfather's come back beside Mama. She's sitting down, completely lost in her thoughts. The dress and the hat are here, on the chair, but my mother's not in them anymore. My grandfather comes closer, sees that her mind's somewhere else, and he moves his cane in front of her eyes, saying: "Wake up, child." My mother blinks, shakes her head. "What were you thinking about?" my grandfather asks. And she, smiling with great effort: "I was thinking about the Pup."

My grandfather sits down beside her again, his chin resting on his cane. He says: "That's a coincidence. I was thinking about him too."

They understand their words. They talk without looking at each other, Mama leaning back in her chair and my grandfather sitting next to her, his chin still resting on his cane. But even like that they understand each other's words, the way Abraham and I can understand each other when we go to see Lucrecia.

I tell Abraham: "Now I'm tecky-tacking." Abraham always walks in front, about three steps ahead of me. Without turning around to look, he says: "Not yet, in a minute." And I say to him: "When I teck somebum hoblows up." Abraham doesn't turn his head but I can hear him laugh softly with a foolish and simple laugh that's like the thread of water that trembles down from the snout of an ox when he's finished drinking. He says: "It must be around five o'clock." He runs a little more and says: "If we go now somebum might hoblow." But I insist: "In any case, there's always tecky-tacking." And he turns to me and starts to run, saying: "All right, then, let's go."

In order to see Lucrecia you have to go through five yards full of trees and bushes. You have to go over the low wall that's green with lizards where the midget with a woman's voice used to sing. Abraham goes running along, shining like a sheet of metal in the strong light, his heels harried by the dog's barking. Then he stops. At that point we're by the window. We say: "Lucrecia," making our voices low as if Lucrecia was sleeping. But she's awake, sitting on the bed, her shoes off, wearing a loose nightgown, white and starched, that reaches down to her ankles.

When we speak, Lucrecia lifts her eyes and makes them turn around the room, fastening a round, large eye like that of a curlew on us. Then she laughs and begins to move toward the center of the room. Her mouth is open and she shows her small, broken teeth. She has a round head, with the hair cut like a man's. When she gets to the center of the room she stops laughing, squats down, and looks at the door until her hands reach her ankles, and she slowly begins to lift her gown, with a calculated slowness, cruel and challenging at the same time. Abraham and I are still looking in the window while Lucrecia lifts up her gown, her lips sticking out in a panting and anxious frown, her big curlew eyes staring and shining. Then we can see her white stomach, which turns deep blue farther down, when she covers her face with the nightgown and stays that way, stretched out in the center of the bedroom, her legs together and tight with a trembling force that comes up from her ankles. All of a sudden she quickly uncovers her face, points at us with her forefinger, and the shining eye pops out in the midst of terrible shrieks that echo all through the house. Then the door of the room opens and the woman comes in shouting: "Why don't you go screw the patience of your own mothers?"

We haven't been to see Lucrecia for days. Now we go to the river along the road to the plantations. If we get out of this early, Abraham will be waiting for me. But my grandfather doesn't move. He's sitting next to Mama with his chin on his cane. I keep watching him, watching his eyes behind his glasses, and he must feel that I'm looking at him, because all of a sudden he gives a deep sigh, shakes himself, and says to my mother in a low, sad voice: "The Pup would have made them come if he had to whip them."

Then he gets up from his chair and walks over to where the dead man is.

It's the second time that I've been in this room. The first time, ten years ago, things were just the same. It's as if they hadn't been touched since then or as if since that remote dawn when he came here to live with Meme he hadn't worried about his life anymore. The papers were in the same place. The table, the few cheap articles of clothing, everything was in the same place it's in today. As if it were yesterday when the Pup and I came to make peace between this man and the authorities.

By that time the banana company had stopped squeezing us and had left Macondo with the rubbish of the rubbish they'd brought us. And with them went the leaf storm, the last traces of what prosperous Macondo had been like in 1915. A ruined village was left here, with four poor, dark stores; occupied by unemployed and angry people who were tormented by a prosperous past and the bitterness of an overwhelming and static present. There was nothing in the future at that time except a gloomy and threatening election Sunday.

Six months before an anonymous note had been found nailed to the door of this house one morning. No one was interested in it and it stayed nailed here for a long time until the final drizzle washed away its dark letters and the paper disappeared, hauled off by the last winds of February. But toward the end of 1918, when the closeness of the elections made the government think about the necessity of keeping the tension of its voters awake and irritated, someone spoke to the new authorities concerning this solitary doctor, about whose existence there would have to be some valid evidence after such a long time. They had to be told that during the first years the Indian woman who lived with him ran a shop that shared in the same prosperity that favored even the most insignificant enterprises in Macondo during those times. One day (no one remembers the date, not even the year) the door

79

of the shop didn't open. It was imagined that Meme and the doctor were still living here, shut up, living on the vegetables they grew themselves in the yard. But in the note that appeared on this corner it said that the physician had murdered his concubine and buried her in the garden, afraid that the town would use her to poison him. The inexplicable thing is that it was said during a time when no one could have had any reason to plot the doctor's death. I think that the authorities had forgotten about his existence until that year when the government reinforced the police and the reserves with men they could trust. Then they dug up the forgotten legend of the anonymous note and the authorities violated these doors, searched the house, dug up the yard, and probed in the privy trying to locate Meme's body. But they couldn't find a trace of her.

On that occasion they would have dragged the doctor out, beaten him, and he most surely would have been one more sacrifice on the public square in the name of official order. But the Pup stepped in; he came to my house and invited me to visit the doctor, certain that I'd be able to get a satisfactory explanation from him.

When we went in the back way we found the ruins of a man abandoned in the hammock. Nothing in this world can be more fearsome than the ruins of a man. And those of this citizen of nowhere who sat up in the hammock when he saw us come in were even worse, and he himself seemed to be covered by the coat of dust that covered everything in the room. His head was steely and his hard yellow eyes still had the powerful inner strength that I had seen in them in my house. I had the impression that if we'd scratched him with our nails his body would have fallen apart, turning into a pile of human sawdust. He'd cut his mustache but he hadn't shaved it off. He'd used shears on his beard so that his chin didn't seem to be sown with hard and vigorous sprouts but with soft, white fuzz. Seeing him in the hammock I thought: *He doesn't look like a man now. Now he looks like a corpse whose eyes still haven't died.*

When he spoke his voice was the same parsimonious ruminant voice that he'd brought to our house. He said that he had nothing to say. He said, as if he thought that we didn't know about it, that the police had violated his doors and had dug in his yard without his consent. But that wasn't a protest. It was only a complaining and melancholy confidence.

As for Meme, he gave us an explanation that might have seemed puerile, but which was said by him with the same accent with which he would have told the truth. He said that Meme had left, that was all. When she closed the shop she began to get restless in the house. She didn't speak to anyone, she had no communication at all with the outside world. He said that one day he saw her packing her bag and he didn't say anything to her. He said that he still didn't say anything when he saw her in her street clothes, high heels, with the suitcase in her hand, standing in the doorway but not speaking, only as if she were showing herself like that so that he would know that she was leaving. "Then," he said, "I got up and gave her the money that was left in the drawer."

I asked him: "How long ago was that, doctor?"

And he said: "You can judge by my hair. She was the one who cut it."

The Pup didn't say much on that visit. From the time he'd entered the room he seemed impressed by the sight of the only man he hadn't met after being in Macondo fifteen years. That time I noticed (and more than ever, maybe because the doctor had cut his mustache) the extraordinary resemblance between those two men. They weren't exact, but they looked like brothers. One was several years older, thinner and more emaciated. But there was the community of features between them that exists between two brothers, even if one looks like the father and the other like the mother. Then I recalled that last night on the veranda. I said:

"This is the Pup, doctor. You promised me you'd visit him once."

He smiled. He looked at the priest and said: "That's right, colonel. I don't know why I didn't." And he continued looking at him, examining him, until the Pup spoke.

"It's never too late for a good beginning," he said. "I'd like to be your friend."

At once I realized that facing the stranger, the Pup had lost his usual strength. He spoke timidly, without the inflexible assurance with which his voice thundered from the pulpit reading the atmospheric predictions of the Bristol Almanac in a transcendental and threatening tone.

That was the first time they'd seen each other. And it was also the last. Still, the doctor's life was prolonged until this morning because the Pup had intervened again in his favor on the night they begged him to take care of the wounded and he wouldn't even open the door, and they shouted that terrible sentence down on him, the fulfillment of which I've now undertaken to prevent.

We were getting ready to leave the house when I remembered something that I'd wanted to ask him for years. I told the Pup I was going to stay awhile with the doctor while he interceded with the authorities. When we were alone I asked him:

"Tell me something, doctor. What was the child?"

He didn't change his expression. "What child, colonel?" he asked. And I said: "Yours. Meme was pregnant when you left my house." And he, tranquil, imperturbable:

"You're right, colonel. I'd even forgotten about that."

My father was silent. Then he said: "The Pup would have made them come if he had to whip them." My father's eyes show a restrained nervousness. And while this waiting goes on, it's been a half hour already (because it must be around three o'clock), I'm worried about the child's perplexity, his absorbed expression, which doesn't seem to be asking anything, his abstract and cold indifference, which makes him just like his father. My son's going to dissolve in the boiling air of this Wednesday just as it happened to Martín nine years ago, when he waved from the train window and disappeared forever. All my sacrifices for this son will be in vain if he keeps on looking like his father. It won't be of any use for me to beg God to make him a man of flesh and blood, one who has volume, weight, and color like other men. Everything will be in vain as long as he has the seeds of his father in his blood.

Five years ago the child didn't have anything of Martín's. Now he's getting to have it all, ever since Genoveva García came back to Macondo with her six children, with two sets of twins among them. Genoveva was fat and old. Blue veins had come out around her eyes, giving a certain look of dirtiness to her face, which had been clean and firm before. She showed a noisy and disordered happiness in the midst of her flock of small white shoes and organdy frills. I knew that Genoveva had run away with the head of a company of puppeteers and I felt some kind of repugnance at seeing those children of hers, who seemed to have automatic movements, as if run by some single central mechanism; small and upsettingly alike, all six with identical shoes and identical frills on their clothing. Genoveva's disorganized happiness seemed painful and sad to me, as did her presence, loaded with urban accessories, in a ruined town that was annihilated by dust. There was something bitter, something inconsolably ridiculous, in her way of moving, of seeming fortunate and of feeling sorry for our way of life, which was so different, she said, from the one she had known in the company of the puppeteers.

Looking at her I remembered other times. I said to her: "You've gotten very fat." And then she became sad. She said: "It must be that memories make a person fat." And she stood there looking closely at the child. She said: "And what happened to the wizard with four buttons?" And I answered her right out, because I knew that she knew: "He went away." And Genoveva said: "And didn't he leave you anything but that?" And I told her no, he'd only left me the child. Genoveva laughed with a loose and vulgar laugh. "He must have been pretty sloppy to make only one child in five years," she said, and she went on, still moving about and cackling in the midst of her confused flock: "And I was mad about him. I swear I would have taken him away from you if it hadn't been that we'd met him at a child's wake. I was very superstitious in those days."

It was before she said good-bye that Genoveva stood looking at the child and said: "He's really just like him. All he needs is the four-button jacket." And from that moment on the child began to look just like his father to me, as if Genoveva had brought on the curse of his identity. On certain occasions I would catch him with his elbows on the table, his head leaning over his left shoulder, and his foggy look turned nowhere. He was just like Martín when he leaned against the carnation pots on the railing and said: "Even if it hadn't been for you, I'd like to spend the rest of my life in Macondo." Sometimes I get the impression that he's going to say it; how could he say it now that he's sitting next to me, silent, touching his nose that's stuffed up with the heat? "Does it hurt you?" I asked him. And he says no, that he was thinking that he couldn't keep glasses on. "You don't have to worry about that," I tell him, and I undo his tie. I say: "When we get home you can rest and have a bath." And then I look toward where my father has just said: "Cataure," calling the oldest of the Guajiros. He's a heavyset and short Indian, who was smoking on the bed, and when he hears his name he lifts his head and looks for my father's face with his small somber eyes. But when my father is about to speak again the steps of the mayor are heard in the back room as he staggers into the bedroom.

XI.

This noon has been terrible for our house. Even though the news of his death was no surprise to me, because I was expecting it for a long time, I couldn't imagine that it would bring on such an upset in my house. Someone had to go to this burial with me and I thought that one would be my wife, especially since my illness three years ago and that afternoon when she found the cane with the silver handle and the wind-up dancer when she was looking through the drawers of my desk. I think that we'd forgotten about the toy by then. But that afternoon we made the mechanism work and the ballerina danced as on other occasions, animated by the music that had been festive before and which then, after the long silence in the drawer, sounded quiet and nostalgic. Adelaida watched it dance and remembered. Then she turned to me, her look moistened by simple sadness:

"Who does it remind you of?" she asked.

And I knew who Adelaida was thinking about, while the toy saddened the room with its worn-out little tune.

"I wonder what's become of him?" my wife asked, remembering, shaken perhaps by the breath of those days when he'd appeared at the door of the room at six in the afternoon and hung the lamp in the doorway.

"He's on the corner," I said. "One of these days he'll die and we'll have to bury him."

Adelaida remained silent, absorbed in the dance of the toy, and I felt infected by her nostalgia. I said to her: "I've always wanted to know who you thought he was the day he came. You set that table because he reminded you of someone."

And Adelaida said with a gray smile:

"You'd laugh at me if I told you who he reminded me of when he stood there in the corner with the ballerina in his hand." And she pointed to the empty space where she'd seen him twenty-two years before, with full boots and a costume that looked like a military uniform.

I thought on that afternoon they'd been reconciled in memory, so today I told my wife to get dressed in black to go with me. But the toy is back in the drawer. The music has lost its effect. Adelaida is wearing herself out now. She's sad, devastated, and she spends hours on end praying in her room. "Only you would have thought of a burial like that," she told me. "After all the misfortunes that befell us, all we needed was that cursed leap year. And then the deluge." I tried to persuade her that my word of honor was involved in this undertaking.

"We can't deny that I owe my life to him," I said.

And she said:

"He's the one who owes his to us. All he did when he saved your life was to repay a debt for eight years of bed, board, and clean clothes."

Then she brought a chair over to the railing. And she must be there still, her eyes foggy with grief and superstition. Her attitude seemed so decided that I tried to calm her down. "All right. In that case I'll go with Isabel," I said. And she didn't answer. She sat there, inviolable, until we got ready to leave and I told her, thinking to please her: "Until we get back, go to the altar and pray for us." Then she turned her head toward the door, saying: "I'm not even going to pray. My prayers will still be useless just as long as that woman comes every Tuesday to ask for a branch of lemon balm." And in her voice there was an obscure and overturned rebellion:

"I'll stay collapsed here until Judgment Day. If the termites haven't eaten up the chair by then."

My father stops, his neck stretched out, listening to the familiar footsteps that are advancing through the back room. Then he forgets what he was going to tell Cataure and tries to turn around, leaning on his cane, but his useless leg fails him in the turn and he's about to fall down, as happened three years ago when he fell into the lemonade bowl, with the noise of the bowl as it rolled along the floor and the clogs and the rocker and the shout of the child, who was the only one who saw him fall.

He's limped ever since then, since then he's dragged the foot that hardened after that week of bitter suffering, from which we thought he'd never recover. Now, seeing him like that, getting his balance back with the help of the mayor, I think that that useless leg holds the secret of the compromise that he's going to fulfill against the will of the town.

Maybe his gratitude goes back to that time. From the time he fell on the veranda, saying that he felt as if he'd been pushed off a tower, and the last two doctors left in Macondo advised him to prepare for a good death. I remember him on the fifth day in bed, shrunken between the sheets; I remember his emaciated body, like the body of the Pup, who'd been carried to the cemetery the year before by all the inhabitants of Macondo in a compressed and moving procession of flowers. Inside the coffin his majesty had the same depth of irremediable and disconsolate abandonment that I saw in the face of my father during those days when the bedroom filled up with his voice and he spoke about that strange soldier who appeared one night in the camp of Colonel Aureliano Buendía during the war of '85, his hat and boots decorated with the skin, teeth, and claws of a tiger, and they asked him: "Who are you?" And the strange soldier didn't answer; and they asked him: "Where do you come from?" And he still didn't answer; and they asked him: "What side are you fighting on?" And they still didn't get any answer from the strange soldier, until an orderly picked up a torch and held it close to his face, examined it for an instant, and exclaimed, scandalized: "Jesus! It's the Duke of Marlborough!"

In the midst of that terrible hallucination, the doctors gave orders to bathe him. It was done. But on the next day you could only see a small change in his stomach. Then the doctors left the house and said that the only thing advisable was to prepare him for a good death..

The bedroom was sunken in a silent atmosphere in which you could hear only the slow and measured flapping of the wings of death, that mysterious flapping that has the smell of a man in the bedrooms of the dying. After Father Angel administered the last rites, many hours passed before anyone moved, looking at the angular profile of the hopeless man. Then the clock struck and my stepmother got ready to give him his spoonful of medicine. That was when we heard the spaced and affirmative footsteps on the veranda. My stepmother held the spoon in the air, stopped murmuring her prayer, and turned to the door, paralyzed by a sudden blush. "I'd recognize those steps even in purgatory," she managed to say at the precise moment that we looked toward the door and saw the doctor. He was on the threshold, looking at us.

I say to my daughter: "The Pup would have made them come even if he had to whip them," and I go over to where the coffin is, thinking: *Since the time the doctor left our house I've been convinced that our acts were ordained by a higher will against which we couldn't have rebelled, even if we tried with all our strength, or even if we assumed the sterile attitude of Adelaida, who shut herself up to pray.*

And while I cover the distance that separates me from the coffin, looking at my men, impassive, sitting on the bed, I feel that I've breathed in the first breath of air that boils up over the dead man, all that bitter matter of fate that destroyed Macondo. I don't think the mayor will delay with the authorization for the burial. I know that outside, on the streets tormented by the heat, people are waiting. I know that there are women in the windows, anxious for a spectacle, and that they stay there, looking out, forgetting that the milk is boiling on the stove and that the rice is dry. But I think that even this last show of rebellion is beyond the possibilities of this crushed and flayed group of men. Their capacity for fight has been broken ever since that Sunday election day when they moved, drew up their plans, and were defeated, and afterward they still were convinced that they were the ones who determined their own acts. But all of that seemed to have been disposed, ordained, channeling the deeds that would lead us step by step to this fateful Wednesday.

Ten years ago, when ruin came down upon us, the collective strength of those who looked for recovery might have been enough for reconstruction. All that was needed was to go out into the fields laid waste by the banana company, clean out the weeds, and start again from scratch. But they'd trained the leaf storm to be impatient, not to believe in either past or future. They'd trained it to believe in the moment and to sate the voracity of its appetite in it. We only needed a short time to realize that the leaf storm had left and that without it reconstruction was impossible. The leaf storm had brought everything and it had taken everything away. After it all that was left was a Sunday in the rubble of a town and the ever-present electoral schemer on Macondo's last night, setting up four demijohns of liquor in the public square at the disposal of the police and the reserves.

If the Pup managed to hold them back that night in spite of the fact that their rebellion was still alive, today he would have been capable of going from house to house armed like a dogcatcher obliging them to bury this man. The Pup held them under an ironclad discipline. Even after the priest died four years ago— one year before my illness—that discipline could be seen in the impassioned way in which they all cut the flowers and shrubs in their gardens and took them to his grave in a final tribute to the Pup.

This man was the only one who didn't go to the burial. The only one, precisely, who owed his life to that unbreakable and contradictory subordination of the town to the priest. Because the night they set out the four demijohns of liquor on the square and Macondo became a town overrun by armed barbarians, a town in terror which buried its dead in a common grave, someone must have remembered that there was a doctor on this corner. That was when they laid the stretchers by the door and shouted to him (because he didn't open up, he spoke from inside); they shouted to him: "Doctor, take care of these wounded people because there aren't enough doctors to go around," and he replied: "Take them somewhere else, I don't know about any of that." And they said to him: "You're the only doctor left. You have to do a charitable act." And he answered (and still hadn't opened the door), imagined by the crowd to be in the middle of the room, the lamp held high, his hard yellow eyes lighted up: "I've forgotten everything I knew about all that. Take them somewhere else," and he stayed there (because the door was never opened) with the door closed, while men and women of Macondo were dying in front of it. The crowd was capable of anything that night. They were getting ready to set fire to the house and reduce its only occupant to ashes. But then the Pup appeared. They say that it was as if he'd been there invisible, standing guard to stop the destruction of the house and the man. "No one will touch this door," they say the Pup said. And they say that was all he said, his arms open as if on a cross, his inexpressive and cold cow-skull face illuminated by the glow of rural fury. And then the impulse was reined in, it changed direction, but it still had sufficient force for them to shout the sentence that would assure the coming of this Wednesday for all the ages.

Walking toward the bed to tell my men to open the door, I think: *He'll be coming any minute now.* And I think that if he doesn't get here in five minutes we'll take the coffin out without any authorization and put the dead man in the street so he'll have to bury him right in front of the house. "Cataure," I say, calling the oldest of my men, and he barely has time to lift his head when I hear the mayor's footsteps coming through the next room.

I know that he's coming straight toward me and I try to turn quickly on my heels, leaning on my cane, but my bad leg fails me and I go forward, sure that I'm going to fall and hit my face against the coffin, when I stumble across his arm and clutch it firmly, and I hear his voice of peaceful stupidity saying: "Don't worry, colonel, I can assure you that nothing will happen." And I think that's how it is, but I know he's saying it to give himself courage. "I don't think anything will happen," I tell him, thinking just the opposite, and he says something about the ceiba trees in the cemetery and hands me the authorization for the burial. Without reading it I fold it, put it in my vest pocket, and tell him: "In any case, whatever happens, it had to happen. It's as if it had been announced in the almanac."

The mayor goes over to the Indians. He tells them to nail up the coffin and open the door. And I see them moving about, looking for the hammer and nails which will remove the sight of that man forever, that unsheltered gentleman from nowhere whom I saw for the last time three years ago beside my convalescent's bed, his head and face cracked by premature decrepitude. He had just rescued me from death then. The same force that had brought him there, that had given him the news of my illness, seemed to be the one which held him up beside my bed saying:

"You just have to exercise that leg a little. You may have to use a cane from now on."

I would ask him two days later what I owed him and he would answer: "You don't owe me anything, colonel. But if you want to do me a favor, throw a little earth on me when morning finds me stiff. That's all I need for the buzzards not to eat me."

In the promise he made me give, in the way he proposed it, in the rhythm of his footsteps on the tile in the room, it was evident that this man had begun to die a long time back, even though three years would pass before that postponed and defective death would be completely realized. That day was today. And I even think that he probably didn't need the noose. A slight breeze would have been enough to extinguish the last glow of life that remained in his hard yellow eyes. I'd sensed all that ever since the night I spoke to him in his little room, before he came here to live with Meme. So when he made me promise what I'm about to do now, I didn't feel upset. I told him simply:

"It's an unnecessary request, doctor. You know me and you must know that I would have buried you over the heads of everybody even if I didn't owe my life to you."

And he, smiling, his hard yellow eyes peaceful for the first time: "That's all very true, colonel. But don't forget that a dead man wouldn't have been able to bury me."

Now no one will be able to correct this shame. The mayor has handed my father the burial order and my father has said: "In any case, whatever happens, it had to happen. It's as if it had been announced in the almanac." And he said it with the same indolence with which he turned himself over to the fate of Macondo, faithful to the trunks where the clothing of all those who died before I was born is kept. Since then everything has gone downhill. Even my stepmother's energy, her ironclad and dominant character have been changed into bitter doubt. She seems more and more distant and silent, and her disillusionment is such that this afternoon she sat down beside the railing and said: "I'll stay collapsed here until Judgment Day."

My father hadn't ever imposed his will on anything again. Only today did he get up to fulfill that shameful promise. He's here, sure that everything will happen with no serious consequences, watching the Guajiros starting to move to open the door and nail up the coffin. I see them coming closer, I stand up, I take the child by the hand and pull the chair toward the window so as not to be seen by the town when they open the door.

The child is puzzled. When I get up he looks me in the face with an indescribable expression, a little upset. But now he's perplexed, beside me, watching the Indians, who are sweating because of the effort to open the bolts. And with a penetrating and sustained lament of rusty metal, the doors open wide. Then I see the street again, the glowing and burning white dust that covers the houses and has given the town the lamentable look of a run-down piece of furniture. It's as if God had declared Macondo

92

unnecessary and had thrown it into the corner where towns that have stopped being of any service to creation are kept.

The child, who at the first moment must have been dazzled by the sudden light (his hand trembled in mine when the door was opened), raises his head suddenly, concentrated, intent, and he asks me: "Did you hear it?" Only then do I realize that in some neighboring courtyard a curlew is telling the time. "Yes," I say. "It must be three o'clock already," and almost at that precise moment the first hammer blow sounds on the nail.

Trying not to listen to the lacerating sound that makes my skin crawl, trying to prevent the child from noticing my confusion, I turn my face to the window and in the next block I see the melancholy and dusty almond trees with our house in the background. Shaken by the invisible breath of destruction, it too is on the eve of a silent and final collapse. All of Macondo has been like that ever since it was squeezed by the banana company. Ivy invades the houses, weeds grow in the alleys, walls crumble, and in the middle of the day a person finds a lizard in her room. Everything has seemed destroyed since we stopped cultivating the rosemary and the nard; since the time an invisible hand cracked the Christmas dishes in the cupboard and put moths to fatten on the clothes that nobody wore anymore. When a door becomes loose there isn't a solicitous hand ready to repair it. My father doesn't have the energy to move the way he did before the collapse that left him limping forever. Señora Rebeca, behind her eternal fan, doesn't bother about anything that might repel the hunger of malevolence that's provoked in her by her sterile and tormented widowhood. Agueda is crippled, overwhelmed by a patient religious illness; and Father Ángel doesn't seem to have any other satisfaction except savoring the persevering indigestion of meatballs every day during his siesta. The only thing that seems unchanged is the song of the twins of Saint Jerome and that mysterious beggar woman who doesn't seem to grow old and who for twenty years has come to the house every Tuesday for a branch of lemon balm. Only the whistle of a yellow, dusty train that doesn't take anyone away breaks the silence four times a day. And at night the toom-toom of the electric plant that the banana company left behind when it left Macondo.

I can see the house through the window and I am aware that my stepmother is there, motionless in her chair, thinking perhaps that before we get back that final wind which will wipe out this town will have passed. Everyone will have gone then except us, because we're tied to this soil by a roomful of trunks where the household goods and clothing of grandparents, my grandparents, are kept, and the canopies that my parents' horses used when they came to Macondo, fleeing from the war. We've been sown into this soil by the memory of the remote dead whose bones can no longer be found twenty fathoms under the earth. The trunks have been in the room ever since the last days of the war; and they'll be there this afternoon when we come back from the burial, if that final wind hasn't passed, the one that will sweep away Macondo, its bedrooms full of lizards and its silent people devastated by memories.

Suddenly my grandfather gets up, leans on his cane, and stretches out his bird head where his glasses seem to be fastened on as if they were part of his face. I think it would be hard for me to wear glasses. With the smallest movement they'd slip off my ears. And thinking about that I tap my nose. Mama looks at me and asks: "Does it hurt you?" And I tell her no, that I was just thinking that I wouldn't be able to wear glasses. And she smiles, breathes deeply, and tells me: "You must be soaked." And she's right; my clothes are burning on my skin, the thick, green corduroy, fastened all the way up, is sticking to my body with sweat and gives me an itchy feeling. "Yes," I say. And my mother leans over me, loosens my tie and fans my collar, saying: "When we get home you can rest and have a bath." "Cataure," I hear.

At that point, through the rear door, the man with the revolver comes in again. When he gets in the doorway he takes off his hat and walks carefully, as if he was afraid of waking up the corpse. But he did it to surprise my grandfather, who falls forward, pushed by the man, staggers, and manages to grab the arm of the same man who'd tried to knock him down. The others have stopped smoking and are still sitting on the bed in a row like four crows on a sawhorse. When the man with the revolver comes in the crows lean over and talk secretly and one of them gets up, goes over to the table, and picks up the box of nails and the hammer.

My grandfather is talking to the man beside the coffin. The man says: "Don't worry, colonel. I can assure you that nothing will happen." And my grandfather says: "I don't think anything will happen." And the man says: "They can bury him on the outside, against the left wall of the cemetery where the ceiba trees are the tallest." Then he gives my grandfather a piece of paper, saying: "You'll see that everything will turn out fine." My grandfather leans on his cane with one hand, takes the paper with the other, and puts it into his vest pocket, where he keeps his small, square gold watch with a chain. Then he says: "In any case, whatever happens, it had to happen. It's as if it had been announced in the almanac."

The man says: "There are some people in the windows, but that's just curiosity. The women always look at anything." But I don't think my grandfather heard him, because he's looking through the window at the street. The man moves then, goes over to the bed, and, fanning himself with his hat, he tells the men: "You can nail it up now. In the meantime, open the door so we can get a breath of air."

The men start to move. One of them leans over the box with the hammer and nails and the others go to the door. My mother gets up. She's sweaty and pale. She pulls her chair, takes me by the hand, and tugs me aside so that the men can get by to open the door.

95

At first they try to turn the bolt, which seems to be soldered to the rusty catches, but they can't move it. It's as if someone were pushing with all his strength from the street side. But when one of the men leans against the door and pounds it, the room is filled with the noise of wood, rusty hinges, locks soldered by time, layer upon layer, and the door opens, enormous, as if a man could go through on another's shoulders; and there's a long creaking of wood and iron that's been awakened. And before we have time to find out what's happened, the light bursts into the room, backward, powerful and perfect, because they've taken away the support that held it for two hundred years with the strength of two hundred oxen, and it falls backward into the room, dragging in the shadow of things in its turbulent fall. The men become brutally visible, like a flash of lightning at noon, and they stumble, and it looks as if they had to hold themselves up so that the light wouldn't knock them down.

When the door opens a curlew begins to sing somewhere in town. Now I can see the street. I can see the bright and burning dust. I can see several men sitting on the opposite sidewalk, their arms folded, looking toward the room. I hear the curlew again and I say to Mama: "Did you hear it?" And she says yes, it must be three o'clock. But Ada told me that curlews sing when they get the smell of a dead man. I'm about to tell my mother just at the moment when I hear the sharp sound of the hammer on the head of the first nail. The hammer pounds, pounds, and fills everything up; it rests a second and pounds again, wounding the wood six times in a row, waking up the long, sad sound of the sleeping boards while my mother, her face turned the other way, looks through the window into the street.

When the hammering is over the song of several curlews can be heard. My grandfather signals his men. They lean over, tip the coffin, while the one who stayed in the corner with his hat says to my grandfather: "Don't worry, colonel." And then my grandfather turns toward the corner, agitated, his neck swollen and purple like that of a fighting cock. But he doesn't say anything. It's the man who speaks again from the corner. He says: "I don't even think there's anyone left in town who remembers this."

At that instant I really feel the quiver in my stomach. *Now I do feel like going out back*, I think; but I see that it's too late now. The men make a last effort; they straighten up, their heels dug into the floor, and the coffin is floating in the light as if they were carrying off a dead ship to be buried.

I think: *Now they'll get the smell. Now all the curlews will start to sing.*

(1955)

97

The Handsomest Drowned
Man in the World

A TALE FOR CHILDREN

The first children who saw the dark and slinky bulge approaching through the sea let themselves think it was an enemy ship. Then they saw it had no flags or masts and they thought it was a whale. But when it washed up on the beach, they removed the clumps of seaweed, the jellyfish tentacles, and the remains of fish and flotsam, and only then did they see that it was a drowned man.

They had been playing with him all afternoon, burying him in the sand and digging him up again, when someone chanced to see them and spread the alarm in the village. The men who carried him to the nearest house noticed that he weighed more than any dead man they had ever known, almost as much as a horse, and they said to each other that maybe he'd been floating too long and the water had got into his bones. When they laid him on the floor they said he'd been taller than all other men because there was barely enough room for him in the house, but they thought that maybe the ability to keep on growing after death was part of the nature of certain drowned men. He had the smell of the sea about him and only his shape gave one to suppose that it was the corpse of a human being, because the skin was covered with a crust of mud and scales.

They did not even have to clean off his face to know that the dead man was a stranger. The village was made up of only twenty-odd wooden houses that had stone courtyards with no flowers and which were spread about on the end of a desertlike cape. There was so little land that mothers always went about with the fear that the wind would carry off their children and the few dead that the years had caused among them had to be thrown off the cliffs. But the sea was calm and bountiful and all the men fitted into seven boats. So when they found the drowned man they simply had to look at one another to see that they were all there.

That night they did not go out to work at sea. While the men went to find out if anyone was missing in neighboring villages, the women stayed behind to care for the drowned man. They took the mud off with grass swabs, they removed the underwater stones entangled in his hair, and they scraped the crust off with tools used for scaling fish. As they were doing that they noticed that the vegetation on him came from faraway oceans and deep water and that his clothes were in tatters, as if he had sailed through labyrinths of coral. They noticed too that he bore his death with pride, for he did not have the lonely look of other drowned men who came out of the sea or that haggard, needy look of men who drowned in rivers. But only when they finished cleaning him off did they become aware of the kind of man he was and it left them breathless. Not only was he the tallest, strongest, most virile, and best built man they had ever seen, but even though they were looking at him there was no room for him in their imagination.

They could not find a bed in the village large enough to lay him on nor was there a table solid enough to use for his wake. The tallest men's holiday pants would not fit him, nor the fattest ones' Sunday shirts, nor the shoes of the one with the biggest feet. Fascinated by his huge size and his beauty, the women then decided to make him some pants from a large piece of sail and a shirt from some bridal brabant linen so that he could continue through his death with dignity. As they sewed, sitting in a circle and gazing at the corpse between stitches, it seemed to them that the wind had never been so steady nor the sea so restless as on that night and they supposed that the change had something to do with the dead man. They thought that if that magnificent man had lived in the village, his house would have had the widest doors, the highest ceiling, and the strongest floor, his bedstead would have been made from a midship frame held together by iron bolts, and his wife would have been the happiest woman. They thought that he would have had so much authority that he could have drawn fish out of the sea simply by calling their names and that he would have put so much work into his land that springs would have burst forth from among the rocks so that he would have been able to plant flowers on the cliffs. They secretly compared him to their own men, thinking that for all their lives theirs were incapable of doing what he could do in one night, and they ended up dismissing them deep in their hearts as the weakest, meanest, and most useless creatures on earth. They were wandering through that maze of fantasy when the oldest woman, who as the oldest had looked upon the drowned man with more compassion than passion, sighed:

"He has the face of someone called Esteban."

It was true. Most of them had only to take another look at him to see that he could not have any other name. The more stubborn among them, who were the youngest, still lived for a few hours with the illusion that when they put his clothes on and he lay among the flowers in patent leather shoes his name might be Lautaro. But it was a vain illusion. There had not been enough canvas, the poorly cut and worse sewn pants were too tight, and the hidden strength of his heart popped the buttons on his shirt. After midnight the whistling of the wind died down and the sea fell into its Wednesday drowsiness. The silence put an end to any last doubts: he was Esteban. The women who had dressed him, who had combed his hair, had cut his nails and shaved him were unable to hold back a shudder of pity when they had to resign themselves to his being dragged along the ground. It was then that they understood how unhappy he must have been with that huge body since it bothered him even after death. They could see him in life, condemned to going through doors sideways, cracking his head on crossbeams, remaining on his feet during visits, not knowing what to do with his soft, pink, sea lion hands while the lady of the house looked for her most resistant chair and begged him, frightened to death, sit here, Esteban, please, and he, leaning against the wall, smiling, don't bother, ma'am, I'm fine where I am, his heels raw and his back roasted from having done the same thing so many times whenever he paid a visit, don't bother, ma'am, I'm fine where I am, just to avoid the embarrassment of breaking up the chair, and never knowing perhaps that the ones who said don't go, Esteban, at least wait till the coffee's ready, were the ones who later on would whisper the big boob finally left, how nice, the handsome fool has gone. That was what the women were thinking beside the body a little before dawn. Later, when they covered his face with a handkerchief so that the light would not bother him, he looked so forever dead, so defenseless, so much like their men that the first furrows of tears opened in their hearts. It was one of the younger ones who began the weeping. The others, coming to, went from sighs to wails, and the more they sobbed the more they felt like weeping, because the drowned man was becoming all the more Esteban for them, and so they wept so much, for he was the most destitute, most peaceful, and most obliging man on earth, poor Esteban. So when the men returned with the news that the drowned man was not from the neighboring villages either, the women felt an opening of jubilation in the midst of their tears.

"Praise the Lord," they sighed, "he's ours!"

The men thought the fuss was only womanish frivolity. Fatigued because of the difficult nighttime inquiries, all they wanted was to get rid of the bother of the newcomer once and for all before the sun grew strong on that arid, windless day. They improvised a litter with the remains of foremasts and gaffs, tying it together with rigging so that it would bear the weight of the body until they reached the cliffs. They wanted to tie the anchor from a cargo ship to him so that he would sink easily into the deepest waves, where fish are blind and divers die of nostalgia, and bad currents would not bring him back to shore, as had happened with other bodies. But the more they hurried, the more the women thought of ways to waste time. They walked about like startled hens, pecking with the sea charms on their breasts, some interfering on one side to put a scapular of the good wind on the drowned man, some on the other side to put a wrist compass on him, and after a great deal of *get away from there, woman, stay out of the way, look, you almost made me fall on top of the dead man*, the men began to feel mistrust in their livers and started grumbling about why so many main-altar decorations for a stranger, because no matter how many nails and holy-water jars he had on him, the sharks would chew him all the same, but the women kept piling on their junk relics, running back and forth, stumbling, while they released in sighs what they did not in tears, so that the men finally exploded with *since when has there ever been such a fuss over a drifting corpse, a drowned nobody, a piece of cold Wednesday meat*. One of the women, mortified by so much lack of care, then removed the handkerchief from the dead man's face and the men were left breathless too.

He was Esteban. It was not necessary to repeat it for them to recognize him. If they had been told Sir Walter Raleigh, even they might have been impressed with his gringo accent, the macaw on his shoulder, his cannibal-killing blunderbuss, but there could be only one Esteban in the world and there he was, stretched out like a sperm whale, shoeless, wearing the pants of an undersized child, and with those stony nails that had to be cut with a knife. They only had to take the handkerchief off his face to see that he was ashamed, that it was not his fault that he was so big or so heavy or so handsome, and if he had known that this was going to happen, he would have looked for a more discreet place to drown in, seriously, I even would have tied the anchor off a galleon around my neck and staggered off a cliff like someone who doesn't like things in order not to be upsetting people now with this Wednesday dead body, as you people say, in order not to be bothering anyone with this filthy piece of cold meat that doesn't have anything to do with me. There was so much truth in his manner that even the most mistrustful men, the ones who felt the bitterness of endless nights at sea fearing that their women would tire of dreaming about them and begin to dream of drowned men, even they and others who were harder still shuddered in the marrow of their bones at Esteban's sincerity.

That was how they came to hold the most splendid funeral they could conceive of for an abandoned drowned man. Some women who had gone to get flowers in the neighboring villages returned with other women who could not believe what they had been told, and those women went back for more flowers when they saw the dead man, and they brought more and more until there were so many flowers and so many people that it was hard to walk about. At the final moment it pained them to return him to the waters as an orphan and they chose a father and mother from among the best people, and aunts and uncles and cousins, so that through him all the inhabitants of the village became kinsmen. Some sailors who heard the weeping from a distance went off course and people heard of one who had himself tied to the mainmast, remembering ancient fables about sirens. While they fought for the privilege of carrying him on their shoulders along the steep escarpment by the cliffs, men and women became aware for the first time of the desolation of their streets, the dryness of their courtyards, the narrowness of their dreams as they faced the splendor and beauty of their drowned man. They let him go without an anchor so that he could come back if he wished and whenever he wished, and they all held their breath for the fraction of centuries the body took to fall into the abyss. They did not need to look at one another to realize that they were no longer all present, that they would never be. But they also knew that everything would be different from then on, that their houses would have wider doors, higher ceilings, and stronger floors so that Esteban's memory could go everywhere without bumping into beams and so that no one in the future would dare whisper the big boob finally died, too bad, the handsome fool has finally died, because they were going to paint their house fronts gay colors to make Esteban's memory eternal and they were going to break their backs digging for springs among the stones and planting flowers on the cliffs so that in future years at dawn the passengers on great liners would awaken, suffocated by the smell of gardens on the high seas, and the captain would have to come down from the bridge in his dress uniform, with his astrolabe, his pole star, and his row of war medals and, pointing to the promontory of roses on the horizon, he would say in fourteen languages, look there, where the wind is so peaceful now that it's gone to sleep beneath the beds, over there, where the sun's so bright that the sunflowers don't know which way to turn, yes, over there, that's Esteban's village.

(1968)

A Very Old Man
with Enormous Wings

A TALE FOR CHILDREN

On the third day of rain they had killed so many crabs inside the house that Pelayo had to cross his drenched courtyard and throw them into the sea, because the newborn child had a temperature all night and they thought it was due to the stench. The world had been sad since Tuesday. Sea and sky were a single ash-gray thing and the sands of the beach, which on March nights glimmered like powdered light, had become a stew of mud and rotten shellfish. The light was so weak at noon that when Pelayo was coming back to the house after throwing away the crabs, it was hard for him to see what it was that was moving and groaning in the rear of the courtyard. He had to go very close to see that it was an old man, a very old man, lying face down in the mud, who, in spite of his tremendous efforts, couldn't get up, impeded by his enormous wings.

Frightened by that nightmare, Pelayo ran to get Elisenda, his wife, who was putting compresses on the sick child, and he took her to the rear of the courtyard. They both looked at the fallen body with mute stupor. He was dressed like a ragpicker. There were only a few faded hairs left on his bald skull and very few teeth in his mouth, and his pitiful condition of a drenched great-grandfather had taken away any sense of grandeur he might have had. His huge buzzard wings, dirty and half-plucked, were forever entangled in the mud. They looked at him so long and so closely that Pelayo and Elisenda very soon overcame their surprise and in the end found him familiar. Then they dared speak to him, and he answered in an incomprehensible dialect with a strong sailor's voice. That was how they skipped over the inconvenience of the wings and quite intelligently concluded that he was a lonely castaway from some foreign ship wrecked by the storm. And yet, they called in a neighbor woman who knew everything about life and death to see him, and all she needed was one look to show them their mistake.

"He's an angel," she told them. "He must have been coming for the child, but the poor fellow is so old that the rain knocked him down."

On the following day everyone knew that a flesh-and-blood angel was held captive in Pelayo's house. Against the judgment of the wise neighbor woman, for whom angels in those times were the fugitive survivors of a celestial conspiracy, they did not have the heart to club him to death. Pelayo watched over him all afternoon from the kitchen, armed with his bailiff's club, and before going to bed he dragged him out of the mud and locked him up with the hens in the wire chicken coop. In the middle of the night, when the rain stopped, Pelayo and Elisenda were still killing crabs. A short time afterward the child woke up without a fever and with a desire to eat. Then they felt magnanimous and decided to put the angel on a raft with fresh water and provisions for three days and leave him to his fate on the high seas. But when they went out into the courtyard with the first light of dawn, they found the whole neighborhood in front of the chicken coop having fun with the angel, without the slightest reverence, tossing him things to eat through the openings in the wire as if he weren't a supernatural creature but a circus animal.

Father Gonzaga arrived before seven o'clock, alarmed at the strange news. By that time onlookers less frivolous than those at dawn had already arrived and they were making all kinds of conjectures concerning the captive's future. The simplest among them thought that he should be named mayor of the world. Others of sterner mind felt that he should be promoted to the rank of five-star general in order to win all wars. Some visionaries hoped that he could be put to stud in order to implant on earth a race of winged wise men who could take charge of the universe. But Father Gonzaga, before becoming a priest, had been a robust woodcutter. Standing by the wire, he reviewed his catechism in an instant and asked them to open the door so that he could take a close look at that pitiful man who looked more like a huge decrepit hen among the fascinated chickens. He was lying in a corner drying his open wings in the sunlight among the fruit peels and breakfast leftovers that the early risers had thrown him. Alien to the impertinences of the world, he only lifted his antiquarian eyes and murmured something in his dialect when Father Gonzaga went into the chicken coop and said good morning to him in Latin. The parish priest had his first suspicion of an imposter when he saw that he did not understand the language of God or know how to greet His ministers. Then he noticed that seen close up he was much too human: he had an unbearable smell of the outdoors, the back side of his wings was strewn with parasites and his main feathers had been mistreated by terrestrial winds, and nothing about him measured up to the proud dignity of angels. Then he came out of the chicken coop and in a brief sermon warned the curious against the risks of being ingenuous. He reminded them that the devil had the bad habit of making use of carnival tricks in order to confuse the unwary. He argued that if wings were not the essential element in determining the difference between a hawk and an airplane, they were even less so in the recognition of angels. Nevertheless, he promised to write a letter to his bishop so that the latter would write to his primate so that the latter would write to the Supreme Pontiff in order to get the final verdict from the highest courts.

His prudence fell on sterile hearts. The news of the captive angel spread with such rapidity that after a few hours the courtyard had the bustle of a marketplace and they had to call in troops with fixed bayonets to disperse the mob that was about to knock the house down. Elisenda, her spine all twisted from sweeping up so much marketplace trash, then got the idea of fencing in the yard and charging five cents admission to see the angel.

The curious came from far away. A traveling carnival arrived with a flying acrobat who buzzed over the crowd several times, but no one paid any attention to him because his wings were not those of an angel but, rather, those of a sidereal bat. The most unfortunate invalids on earth came in search of health: a poor woman who since childhood had been counting her heartbeats and had run out of numbers; a Portuguese man who couldn't sleep because the noise of the stars disturbed him; a sleepwalker who got up at night to undo the things he had done while awake; and many others with less serious ailments. In the midst of that shipwreck disorder that made the earth tremble, Pelayo and Elisenda were happy with fatigue, for in less than a week they had crammed their rooms with money and the line of pilgrims waiting their turn to enter still reached beyond the horizon.

The angel was the only one who took no part in his own act. He spent his time trying to get comfortable in his borrowed nest, befuddled by the hellish heat of the oil lamps and sacramental candles that had been placed along the wire. At first they tried to make him eat some mothballs, which, according to the wisdom of the wise neighbor woman, were the food prescribed for angels. But he turned them down, just as he turned down the papal lunches that the penitents brought him, and they never found out whether it was because he was an angel or because he was an old man that in the end he ate nothing but eggplant mush. His only supernatural virtue seemed to be patience. Especially during the first days, when the hens pecked at him, searching for the stellar parasites that proliferated in his wings, and the cripples pulled out feathers to touch their defective parts with, and even the most merciful threw stones at him, trying to get him to rise so they could see him standing. The only time they succeeded in arousing him was when they burned his side with an iron for branding steers, for he had been motionless for so many hours that they thought he was dead. He awoke with a start, ranting in his hermetic language and with tears in his eyes, and he flapped his wings a couple of times, which brought on a whirlwind of chicken dung and lunar dust and a gale of panic that did not seem to be of this world. Although many thought that his reaction had been one not of rage but of pain, from then on they were careful not to annoy him, because the majority understood that his passivity was not that of a hero taking his ease but that of a cataclysm in repose.

Father Gonzaga held back the crowd's frivolity with formulas of maidservant inspiration while awaiting the arrival of a final judgment on the nature of the captive. But the mail from Rome showed no sense of urgency. They spent their time finding out if the prisoner had a navel, if his dialect had any connection with Aramaic, how many times he could fit on the head of a pin, or whether he wasn't just a Norwegian with wings. Those meager letters might have come and gone until the end of time if a providential event had not put an end to the priest's tribulations.

It so happened that during those days, among so many other carnival attractions, there arrived in town the traveling show of the woman who had been changed into a spider for having disobeyed her parents. The admission to see her was not only less than the admission to see the angel, but people were permitted to ask her all manner of questions about her absurd state and to examine her up and down so that no one would ever doubt the truth of her horror. She was a frightful tarantula the size of a ram and with the head of a sad maiden. What was most heart-rending, however, was not her outlandish shape but the sincere affliction with which she recounted the details of her misfortune. While still practically a child she had sneaked out of her parents' house to go to a dance, and while she was coming back through the woods after having danced all night without permission, a fearful thunderclap rent the sky in two and through the crack came the lightning bolt of brimstone that changed her into a spider. Her only nourishment came from the meatballs that charitable souls chose to toss into her mouth. A spectacle like that, full of so much human truth and with such a fearful lesson, was bound to defeat without even trying that of a haughty angel who scarcely deigned to look at mortals. Besides, the few miracles attributed to the angel showed a certain mental disorder, like the blind man who didn't recover his sight but grew three new teeth, or the paralytic who didn't get to walk but almost won the lottery, and the leper whose sores sprouted sunflowers. Those consolation miracles, which were more like mocking fun, had already ruined the angel's reputation when the woman who had been changed into a spider finally crushed him completely. That was how Father Gonzaga was cured forever of his insomnia and Pelayo's courtyard went back to being as empty as during the time it had rained for three days and crabs walked through the bedrooms.

The owners of the house had no reason to lament. With the money they saved they built a two-story mansion with balconies and gardens and high netting so that crabs wouldn't get in during the winter, and with iron bars on the windows so that angels wouldn't get in. Pelayo also set up a rabbit warren close to town and gave up his job as bailiff for good, and Elisenda bought some satin pumps with high heels and many dresses of iridescent silk, the kind worn on Sunday by the most desirable women in those times. The chicken coop was the only thing that didn't receive any attention. If they washed it down with creolin and burned tears of myrrh inside it every so often, it was not in homage to the angel but to drive away the dungheap stench that still hung everywhere like a ghost and was turning the new house into an old one. At first, when the child learned to walk, they were careful that he did not get too close to the chicken coop. But then they began to lose their fears and got used to the smell, and before the child got his second teeth he'd gone inside the chicken coop to play, where the wires were falling apart. The angel was no less standoffish with him than with other mortals, but he tolerated the most ingenious infamies with the patience of a dog who had no illusions. They both came down with chicken-pox at the same time. The doctor who took care of the child couldn't resist the temptation to listen to the angel's heart, and he found so much whistling in the heart and so many sounds in his kidneys that it seemed impossible for him to be alive. What surprised him most, however, was the logic of his wings. They seemed so natural on that completely human organism that he couldn't understand why other men didn't have them too.

When the child began school it had been some time since the sun and rain had caused the collapse of the chicken coop. The angel went dragging himself about here and there like a stray dying man. They would drive him out of the bedroom with a broom and a moment later find him in the kitchen. He seemed to be in so many places at the same time that they grew to think that he'd been duplicated, that he was reproducing himself all through the house, and the exasperated and unhinged Elisenda shouted that it was awful living in that hell full of angels. He could scarcely eat and his antiquarian eyes had also become so foggy that he went about bumping into posts. All he had left were the bare cannulae of his last feathers. Pelayo threw a blanket over him and extended him the charity of letting him sleep in the shed, and only then did they notice that he had a temperature at night, and was delirious with the tongue twisters of an old Norwegian. That was one of the few times they became alarmed, for they thought he was going to die and not even the wise neighbor woman had been able to tell them what to do with dead angels.

And yet he not only survived his worst winter, but seemed improved with the first sunny days. He remained motionless for several days in the farthest corner of the courtyard, where no one would see him, and at the beginning of December some large, stiff feathers began to grow on his wings, the feathers of a scarecrow, which looked more like another misfortune of decrepitude. But he must have known the reason for those changes, for he was quite careful that no one should notice them, that no one should hear the sea chanteys that he sometimes sang under the stars. One morning Elisenda was cutting some bunches of onions for lunch when a wind that seemed to come from the high seas blew into the kitchen. Then she went to the window and caught the angel in his first attempts at flight. They were so clumsy that his fingernails opened a furrow in the vegetable patch and he was on the point of knocking the shed down with the ungainly flapping that slipped on the light and couldn't get a grip on the air. But he did manage to gain altitude. Elisenda let out a sigh of relief, for herself and for him, when she saw him pass over the last houses, holding himself up in some way with the risky flapping of a senile vulture. She kept watching him even when she was through cutting the onions and she kept on watching until it was no longer possible for her to see him, because then he was no longer an annoyance in her life but an imaginary dot on the horizon of the sea.

(1968)

Blacamán the Good,
Vendor of Miracles

From the first Sunday I saw him he reminded me of a bullring mule, with his white suspenders that were backstitched with gold thread, his rings with colored stones on every finger, and his braids of jingle bells, standing on a table by the docks of Santa María del Darién in the middle of the flasks of specifics and herbs of consolation that he prepared himself and hawked through the towns along the Caribbean with his wounded shout, except that at that time he wasn't trying to sell any of that Indian mess but was asking them to bring him a real snake so that he could demonstrate on his own flesh an antidote he had invented, the only infallible one, ladies and gentlemen, for the bites of serpents, tarantulas, and centipedes plus all manner of poisonous mammals. Someone who seemed quite impressed by his determination managed to get a bushmaster of the worst kind somewhere (the snake that kills by poisoning the respiration) and brought it to him in a bottle, and he uncorked it with such eagerness that we all thought he was going to eat it, but as soon as the creature felt itself free it jumped out of the bottle and struck him on the neck, leaving him right then and there without any wind for his oratory and with barely enough time to take the antidote, and the vest-pocket pharmacist tumbled down into the crowd and rolled about on the ground, his huge body wasted away as if he had nothing inside of it, but laughing all the while with all of his gold teeth. The hubbub was so great that a cruiser from the north that had been docked there for twenty years on a goodwill mission declared a quarantine so that the snake poison wouldn't get on board, and the people who were sanctifying Palm Sunday came out of church with their blessed palms, because no one wanted to miss the show of the poisoned man, who had already begun to puff up with the air of death and was twice as fat as he'd been before, giving off a froth of gall through his mouth and panting through his pores, but still laughing with so much life that the jingle bells tinkled all over his body. The swelling snapped the laces of his leggings and the seams of his clothes, his fingers grew purple from the pressure of the rings, he turned the color of venison in brine, and from his rear end came a hint of the last moments of death, so that everyone who had seen a person bitten by a snake knew that he was rotting away before dying and that he would be so crumpled up that they'd have to pick him up with a shovel to put him into a sack, but they also thought that even in his sawdust state he'd keep on laughing. It was so incredible that the marines came up on deck to take colored pictures of him with long-distance lenses, but the women who'd come out of church blocked their intentions by covering the dying man with a blanket and laying blessed palms on top of him, some because they didn't want the soldiers to profane the body with their Adventist instruments, others because they were afraid to continue looking at that idolater who was ready to die dying with laughter, and others because in that way perhaps his soul at least would not be poisoned. Everybody had given him up for dead when he pushed aside the palms with one arm, still half-dazed and not completely recovered from the bad moment he'd had, but he set the table up without anyone's help, climbed on it like a crab once more, and there he was again, shouting that his antidote was

114

nothing but the hand of God in a bottle, as we had all seen with our own eyes, but it only cost two cuartillos because he hadn't invented it as an item for sale but for the good of all humanity, and as soon as he said that, ladies and gentlemen, I only ask you not to crowd around, there's enough for everybody.

They crowded around, of course, and they did well to do so, because in the end there wasn't enough for everybody. Even the admiral from the cruiser bought a bottle, convinced by him that it was also good for the poisoned bullets of anarchists, and the sailors weren't satisfied with just taking colored pictures of him up on the table, pictures they had been unable to take of him dead, but they had him signing autographs until his arm was twisted with cramps. It was getting to be night and only the most perplexed of us were left by the docks when with his eyes he searched for someone with the look of an idiot to help him put the bottles away, and naturally he spotted me. It was like the look of destiny, not just mine, but his too, for that was more than a century ago and we both remember it as if it had been last Sunday. What happened was that we were putting his circus drugstore into that trunk with purple straps that looked more like a scholar's casket, when he must have noticed some light inside of me that he hadn't seen in me before, because he asked me in a surly way who are you, and I answered that I was an orphan on both sides whose papa hadn't died, and he gave out with laughter that was louder than what he had given with the poison and then he asked me what do you do for a living, and I answered that I didn't do anything except stay alive, because nothing else was worth the trouble, and still weeping with laughter he asked me what science in the world do you most want to learn, and that was the only time I answered the truth without any fooling, I wanted to be a fortune-teller, and then he didn't laugh again but told me as if thinking out loud that I didn't need much for that because I already had the hardest thing to learn, which was my face of an idiot. That same night he spoke to my father and for one real and two cuartillos and a deck of cards that foretold adultery he bought me forevermore.

That was what Blacamán was like, Blacamán the Bad, because I'm Blacamán the Good. He was capable of convincing an astronomer that the month of February was nothing but a herd of invisible elephants, but when his good luck turned on him he became a heart-deep brute. In his days of glory he had been an embalmer of viceroys, and they say that he gave them faces with such authority that for many years they went on governing better than when they were alive, and that no one dared bury them until he gave them back their dead-man look, but his prestige was ruined by the invention of an endless chess game that drove a chaplain mad and brought on two illustrious suicides, and so he was on the decline, from an interpreter of dreams to a birthday hypnotist, from an extractor of molars by suggestion to a market-place healer; therefore, at the time we met, people were already looking at him askance, even the freebooters. We drifted along with our trick stand and life was an eternal uncertainty as we tried to sell escape suppositories that turned smugglers transparent, furtive drops that baptized wives threw into the soup to instill the fear of God in Dutch husbands, and anything you might want to buy of your own free will, ladies and gentlemen, because this isn't a command, it's advice, and, after all, happiness isn't an obligation either. Nevertheless, as much as we died with laughter at his witticisms, the truth is that it was quite hard for us to manage enough to eat, and his last hope was founded on my vocation as a fortune-teller. He shut me up in the sepulchral trunk disguised as a Japanese and bound with starboard chains so that I could attempt to foretell what I could while he disemboweled the grammar book looking for the best way to convince the world of my new science, and here, ladies and gentlemen, you have this child tormented by Ezequiel's glowworms, and those of you who've been standing there with faces of disbelief, let's see if you dare ask him when you're going to die, but I was never able even to guess what day it was at that time, so he gave up on me as a soothsayer because the drowsiness of digestion disturbs your prediction gland, and after whacking me over the head for good luck, he decided to take me to my father and get his money back. But at that time he happened to find a practical application for the electricity of suffering, and he set about building a sewing machine that ran connected by cupping glasses to the part of the body where there was a pain. Since I spent the night moaning over the whacks he'd given me to conjure away misfortune, he had to keep me on as the one who could test his invention, and so our return was delayed and he was getting back his good humor until the machine worked so well that it not only sewed better than a novice nun but also embroidered birds or astromelias according to the position and intensity of the pain. That was what we were up to, convinced of our triumph over bad luck, when the news reached us that in Philadelphia the commander of the cruiser had tried to repeat the experiment with the antidote and that he'd been changed into a glob of admiral jelly in front of his staff.

He didn't laugh again for a long time. We fled through Indian passes and the more lost we became, the clearer the news reached us that the marines had invaded the country under the pretext of exterminating yellow fever and were going about beheading every inveterate or eventual potter they found in their path, and not only the natives, out of precaution, but also the Chinese, for distraction, the Negroes, from habit, and the Hindus, because they were snake charmers, and then they wiped out the flora and fauna and all the mineral wealth they were able to because their specialists in our affairs had taught them that the people along the Caribbean had the ability to change their nature in order to confuse gringos. I couldn't understand where that fury came from or why we were so frightened until we found ourselves safe and sound in the eternal winds of La Guajira, and only then did he have the courage to confess to me that his antidote was nothing but rhubarb and turpentine and that he'd paid a drifter two cuartillos to bring him that bushmaster with all the poison gone. We stayed in the ruins of a colonial mission, deluded by the hope that some smugglers would pass, because they were men to be trusted and the only ones capable of venturing out under the mercurial sun of those salt flats. At first we ate smoked salamanders and flowers from the ruins and we still had enough spirit to laugh when we tried to eat his boiled leggings, but finally we even ate the water cobwebs from the cisterns and only then did we realize how much we missed the world. Since I didn't know of any recourse against death at that time, I simply lay down to wait for it where it would hurt me least, while he was delirious remembering a woman who was so tender that she could pass through walls just by sighing, but that contrived recollection was also a trick of his genius to fool death with lovesickness. Still, at the moment we should have died, he came to me more alive than ever and spent the whole night watching over my agony, thinking with such great strength that I still haven't been able to tell whether what was whistling through the ruins was the wind or his thoughts, and before dawn he told me with the same voice and the same determination of past times that now he knew the truth, that I was the one who had twisted up his luck again, so get your pants ready, because the same way as you twisted it up for me, you're going to straighten it out.

That was when I lost the little affection I had for him. He took óff the last rags I had on, rolled me up in some barbed wire, rubbed rock salt on the sores, put me in brine from my own waters, and hung me by the ankles for the sun to flay me, and he kept on shouting that all that mortification wasn't enough to pacify his persecutors. Finally he threw me to rot in my own misery inside the penance dungeon where the colonial missionaries regenerated heretics, and with the perfidy of a ventriloquist, which he still had more than enough of, he began to imitate the voices of edible animals, the noise of ripe beets, and the sound of fresh springs so as to torture me with the illusion that I was dying of indigence in the midst of paradise. When the smugglers finally supplied him, he came down to the dungeon to give me something to eat so that I wouldn't die, but then he made me pay for that charity by pulling out my nails with pliers and filing my teeth down with a grindstone, and my only consolation was the wish that life would give me time and the good fortune to be quit of so much infamy with even worse martyrdoms. I myself was surprised that I could resist the plague of my own putrefaction and he kept throwing the leftovers of his meals onto me and tossed pieces of rotten lizards and hawks into the corners so that the air of the dungeon would end up poisoning me. I don't know how much time had passed when he brought me the carcass of a rabbit in order to show me that he preferred throwing it away to rot rather than giving it to me to eat, but my patience only went so far and all I had left was rancor, so I grabbed the rabbit by the ears and flung it against the wall with the illusion that it was he and not the animal that was going to explode, and then it happened, as if in a dream. The rabbit not only revived with a squeal of fright, but came back to my hands, hopping through the air.

That was how my great life began. Since then I've gone through the world drawing the fever out of malaria victims for two pesos, visioning blind men for four-fifty, draining the water from dropsy victims for eighteen, putting cripples back together for twenty pesos if they were that way from birth, for twenty-two if they were that way because of an accident or a brawl, for twenty-five if they were that way because of wars, earthquakes, infantry landings, or any other kind of public calamity, taking care of the common sick at wholesale according to a special arrangement, madmen according to their theme, children at half price, and idiots out of gratitude, and who dares say that I'm not a philanthropist, ladies and gentlemen, and now, yes, sir, commandant of the twentieth fleet, order your boys to take down the barricades and let suffering

humanity pass, lepers to the left, epileptics to the right, cripples
where they won't get in the way, and there in the back the least
urgent cases, only please don't crowd in on me because then I
won't be responsible if the sicknesses get all mixed up and people
are cured of what they don't have, and keep the music playing
until the brass boils, and the rockets firing until the angels burn,
and the liquor flowing until ideas are killed, and bring on the
wenches and the acrobats, the butchers and the photographers, and
all at my expense, ladies and gentlemen, for here ends the evil
fame of the Blacamáns and the universal tumult starts. That's how
I go along putting them to sleep with the techniques of a congress-
man in case my judgment fails and some turn out worse than
they were before on me. The only thing I don't do is revive the
dead, because as soon as they open their eyes they're murderous
with rage at the one who disturbed their state, and when it's all
done, those who don't commit suicide die again of disillusionment.
At first I was pursued by a group of wise men investigating the
legality of my industry, and when they were convinced, they
threatened me with the hell of Simon Magus and recommended a
life of penitence so that I could get to be a saint, but I answered
them, with no disrespect for their authority, that it was precisely
along those lines that I had started. The truth is that I'd gain
nothing by being a saint after being dead, an artist is what I
am, and the only thing I want is to be alive so I can keep going
along at donkey level in this six-cylinder touring car I bought
from the marines' consul, with this Trinidadian chauffeur who
was a baritone in the New Orleans pirates' opera, with my genuine
silk shirts, my Oriental lotions, my topaz teeth, my flat straw hat,
and my bicolored buttons, sleeping without an alarm clock, dancing with beauty queens, and leaving them hallucinated with my
dictionary rhetoric, and with no flutter in my spleen if some Ash
Wednesday my faculties wither away, because in order to go on
with this life of a minister, all I need is my idiot face, and I have
more than enough with the string of shops I own from here to

beyond the sunset, where the same tourists who used to go around collecting from us through the admiral, now go stumbling after my autographed pictures, almanacs with my love poetry, medals with my profile, bits of my clothing, and all of that without the glorious plague of spending all day and all night sculpted in equestrian marble and shat on by swallows like the fathers of our country.

It's a pity that Blacamán the Bad can't repeat this story so that people will see that there's nothing invented in it. The last time anyone saw him in this world he'd lost even the studs of his former splendor, and his soul was a shambles and his bones in disorder from the rigors of the desert, but he still had enough jingle bells left to reappear that Sunday on the docks of Santa María del Darién with his eternal sepulchral trunk, except that this time he wasn't trying to sell any antidotes, but was asking in a voice cracking with emotion for the marines to shoot him in a public spectacle so that he could demonstrate on his own flesh the life-restoring properties of this supernatural creature, ladies and gentlemen, and even though you have more than enough right not to believe me after suffering so long from my evil tricks as a deceiver and falsifier, I swear on the bones of my mother that this proof today is nothing from the other world, merely the humble truth, and in case you have any doubts left, notice that I'm not laughing now the way I used to, but holding back a desire to cry. How convincing he must have been, unbuttoning his shirt, his eyes drowning with tears, and giving himself mule kicks on his heart to indicate the best place for death, and yet the marines didn't dare shoot, out of fear that the Sunday crowd would discover their loss of prestige. Someone who may not have forgotten the blacamanipulations of past times managed, no one knew how, to get and bring him in a can enough *barbasco* roots to bring to the surface all the corvinas in the Caribbean, and he opened it with great desire, as if he really was going to eat them, and, indeed, he did eat them, ladies and gentlemen, but please don't be moved or pray for the repose of my soul, because this death is nothing but a visit. That time he was so honest that he didn't break into operatic death rattles, but got off the table like a crab, looked on the ground for the most worthy place to lie down after some hesitation, and from there he looked at me as he would have at a mother and exhaled his last breath in his own arms, still holding back his manly tears all twisted up by the tetanus of eternity. That was the only time, of course, that my science failed me. I put him in that trunk of premonitory size where there was room for him laid out. I had a requiem mass sung for him which cost me fifty four-peso doubloons, because the officiant was dressed in gold and there were also three seated bishops. I had the mausoleum of an emperor built for him on a hill exposed to the best seaside weather, with a chapel just for him and an iron plaque on which there was written in Gothic capitals HERE LIES BLACAMÁN THE DEAD, BADLY CALLED THE BAD, DECEIVER OF MARINES AND VICTIM OF SCIENCE, and when those honors were sufficient for me to do justice to his virtues, I began to get my revenge for his infamy, and then I revived him inside the armored tomb and left him there rolling about in horror. That was long before the fire ants devoured Santa María del Darién, but the mausoleum is still intact on the hill in the shadow of the dragons that climb up to sleep in the Atlantic winds, and every time I pass through here I bring him an automobile load of roses and my heart pains with pity for his virtues, but then I put my ear to the plaque to hear him weeping in the ruins of the crumbling trunk, and if by chance he has died again, I bring him back to life once more, for the beauty of the punishment is that he will keep on living in his tomb as long as I'm alive, that is, forever.

(1968)

The Last Voyage
of the Ghost Ship

Now they're going to see who I am, he said to himself in his
strong new man's voice, many years after he had first seen the
huge ocean liner without lights and without any sound which
passed by the village one night like a great uninhabited palace,
longer than the whole village and much taller than the steeple
of the church, and it sailed by in the darkness toward the colonial
city on the other side of the bay that had been fortified against
buccaneers, with its old slave port and the rotating light, whose
gloomy beams transfigured the village into a lunar encampment of
glowing houses and streets of volcanic deserts every fifteen seconds,
and even though at that time he'd been a boy without a man's
strong voice but with his mother's permission to stay very late on
the beach to listen to the wind's night harps, he could still remember, as if still seeing it, how the liner would disappear when
the light of the beacon struck its side and how it would reappear
when the light had passed, so that it was an intermittent ship
sailing along, appearing and disappearing, toward the mouth of
the bay, groping its way like a sleepwalker for the buoys that
marked the harbor channel until something must have gone wrong
with the compass needle, because it headed toward the shoals,
ran aground, broke up, and sank without a single sound, even

though a collision against the reefs like that should have produced a crash of metal and the explosion of engines that would have frozen with fright the soundest-sleeping dragons in the prehistoric jungle that began with the last streets of the village and ended on the other side of the world, so that he himself thought it was a dream, especially the next day, when he saw the radiant fishbowl of the bay, the disorder of colors of the Negro shacks on the hills above the harbor, the schooners of the smugglers from the Guianas loading their cargoes of innocent parrots whose craws were full of diamonds, he thought, I fell asleep counting the stars and I dreamed about that huge ship, of course, he was so convinced that he didn't tell anyone nor did he remember the vision again until the same night on the following March when he was looking for the flash of dolphins in the sea and what he found was the illusory liner, gloomy, intermittent, with the same mistaken direction as the first time, except that then he was so sure he was awake that he ran to tell his mother and she spent three weeks moaning with disappointment, because your brain's rotting away from doing so many things backward, sleeping during the day and going out at night like a criminal, and since she had to go to the city around that time to get something comfortable where she could sit and think about her dead husband, because the rockers on her chair had worn out after eleven years of widowhood, she took advantage of the occasion and had the boatman go near the shoals so that her son could see what he really saw in the glass of the sea, the lovemaking of manta rays in a springtime of sponges, pink snappers and blue corvinas diving into the other wells of softer waters that were there among the waters, and even the wandering hairs of victims of drowning in some colonial shipwreck, no trace of sunken liners or anything like it, and yet he was so pigheaded that his mother promised to watch with him the next March, absolutely, not knowing that the only thing absolute in her future now was an easy chair from the days of Sir Francis Drake which she had bought at an auction in a Turk's store, in which she sat down to rest that same night, sighing, oh, my poor Olofernos, if you could only see how nice it is to think about you on this velvet lining and this brocade from the casket of a queen, but the more she brought back the memory of her dead husband, the more the blood in her heart bubbled up and turned to chocolate, as if instead of sitting down she were running, soaked from chills and fevers and her breathing full of earth, until he returned at dawn and found her dead in the easy chair, still warm, but half rotted away as after a snakebite, the same as happened afterward to four other women before the murderous chair was thrown into the sea, far away where it wouldn't bring evil to anyone, because it had been used so much over the centuries that its faculty for giving rest had been used up, and so he had to grow accustomed to his miserable routine of an orphan who was pointed out by everyone as the son of the widow who had brought the throne of misfortune into the village, living not so much from public charity as from the fish he stole out of boats, while his voice was becoming a roar, and not remembering his visions of past times anymore until another night in March when he chanced to look seaward and suddenly, good Lord, there it is, the huge asbestos whale, the behemoth beast, come see it, he shouted madly, come see it, raising such an uproar of dogs' barking and women's panic that even the oldest men remembered the frights of their great-grandfathers and crawled under their beds, thinking that William Dampier had come back, but those who ran into the street didn't make the effort to see the unlikely apparatus which at that instant was lost again in the east and raised up in its annual disaster, but they covered him with blows and left him so twisted that it was then he said to himself, drooling with rage, now they're going to see who I am, but he took care not to share his determination with anyone, but spent the whole year with the fixed idea, now they're going to see who I am, waiting for it to be the eve of the apparition once more in order to do what he did, which was steal a boat, cross the bay, and spend the evening waiting for his great moment in the inlets of the slave port, in the human brine of the Caribbean, but so absorbed in his adventure that he didn't stop as he always did in front of the Hindu shops to look at the ivory mandarins carved from the whole tusk of an elephant, nor did he make fun of the Dutch Negroes in their orthopedic velocipedes, nor was he frightened as at other times of the copper-skinned Malayans, who had gone around the world enthralled by the chimera of a secret tavern where they sold roast filets of Brazilian women, because he wasn't aware of anything until night came over him with all the weight of the stars and the jungle exhaled a sweet fragrance of gardenias and rotten salamanders, and there he was, rowing in the stolen boat toward the mouth of the bay, with the lantern out so as not to alert the customs police, idealized every fifteen seconds by the green wing flap of the beacon and turned human once more by the darkness, knowing that he was getting close to the buoys that marked the harbor channel, not only because its oppressive glow was getting more intense, but because the breathing of the water was becoming sad, and he rowed like that, so wrapped up in himself, that he didn't know where the fearful shark's breath that suddenly reached him came from or why the night became dense, as if the stars had suddenly died, and it was because the liner was there, with all of its inconceivable size, Lord, bigger than any other big thing in the world and darker than any other dark thing on land or sea, three hundred thousand tons of shark smell passing so close to the boat that he could see the seams of the steel precipice, without a single light in the infinite portholes, without a sigh from the engines, without a soul, and carrying its own circle of silence with it, its own dead air, its halted time, its errant sea in which a whole world of drowned animals floated, and suddenly it all disappeared with the flash of the beacon and for an instant it was the diaphanous Caribbean once more, the March night, the everyday air of the pelicans, so he stayed alone among the buoys, not knowing what to do, asking himself, startled, if perhaps he wasn't dreaming while

he was awake, not just now but the other times too, but no sooner
had he asked himself than a breath of mystery snuffed out the
buoys, from the first to the last, so that when the light of the
beacon passed by the liner appeared again and now its compasses
were out of order, perhaps not even knowing what part of the
ocean sea it was in, groping for the invisible channel but actually
heading for the shoals, until he got the overwhelming revelation
that that misfortune of the buoys was the last key to the enchant-
ment and he lighted the lantern in the boat, a tiny red light that
had no reason to alarm anyone in the watchtowers but which
would be like a guiding sun for the pilot, because, thanks to it,
the liner corrected its course and passed into the main gate of the
channel in a maneuver of lucky resurrection, and then all the lights
went on at the same time so that the boilers wheezed again, the
stars were fixed in their places, and the animal corpses went to the
bottom, and there was a clatter of plates and a fragrance of laurel
sauce in the kitchens, and one could hear the pulsing of the
orchestra on the moon decks and the throbbing of the arteries of
high-sea lovers in the shadows of the staterooms, but he still
carried so much leftover rage in him that he would not let himself be confused by emotion or be frightened by the miracle, but
said to himself with more decision than ever, now they're going
to see who I am, the cowards, now they're going to see, and instead of turning aside so that the colossal machine would not
charge into him, he began to row in front of it, because now they
really are going to see who I am, and he continued guiding the
ship with the lantern until he was so sure of its obedience that he
made it change course from the direction of the docks once more,
took it out of the invisible channel, and led it by the halter as if it
were a sea lamb toward the lights of the sleeping village, a living
ship, invulnerable to the torches of the beacon, that no longer
made it invisible but made it aluminum every fifteen seconds, and
the crosses of the church, the misery of the houses, the illusion
began to stand out, and still the ocean liner followed behind him,

following his will inside of it, the captain asleep on his heart side, the fighting bulls in the snow of their pantries, the solitary patient in the infirmary, the orphan water of its cisterns, the unredeemed pilot who must have mistaken the cliffs for the docks, because at that instant the great roar of the whistle burst forth, once, and he was soaked with the downpour of steam that fell on him, again, and the boat belonging to someone else was on the point of capsizing, and again, but it was too late, because there were the shells of the shoreline, the stones of the streets, the doors of the disbelievers, the whole village illuminated by the lights of the fearsome liner itself, and he barely had time to get out of the way to make room for the cataclysm, shouting in the midst of the confusion, there it is, you cowards, a second before the huge steel cask shattered the ground and one could hear the neat destruction of ninety thousand five hundred champagne glasses breaking, one after the other, from stem to stern, and then the light came out and it was no longer a March dawn but the noon of a radiant Wednesday, and he was able to give himself the pleasure of watching the disbelievers as with open mouths they contemplated the largest ocean liner in this world and the other aground in front of the church, whiter than anything, twenty times taller than the steeple and some ninety-seven times longer than the village, with its name engraved in iron letters, *Halál-csillag,* and the ancient and languid waters of the seas of death dripping down its sides.

(1968)

Monologue of Isabel Watching
It Rain in Macondo

Winter fell one Sunday when people were coming out of church. Saturday night had been suffocating. But even on Sunday morning nobody thought it would rain. After mass, before we women had time to find the catches on our parasols, a thick, dark wind blew, which with one broad, round swirl swept away the dust and hard tinder of May. Someone next to me said: "It's a water wind." And I knew it even before then. From the moment we came out onto the church steps I felt shaken by a slimy feeling in my stomach. The men ran to the nearby houses with one hand on their hats and a handkerchief in the other, protecting themselves against the wind and the dust storm. Then it rained. And the sky was a gray, jellyish substance that flapped its wings a hand away from our heads.

During the rest of the morning my stepmother and I were sitting by the railing, happy that the rain would revive the thirsty rosemary and nard in the flowerpots after seven months of intense summer and scorching dust. At noon the reverberation of the earth stopped and a smell of turned earth, of awakened and renovated vegetation mingled with the cool and healthful odor of the rain in the rosemary. My father said at lunchtime: "When it rains in May, it's a sign that there'll be good tides." Smiling, crossed by the luminous thread of the new season, my stepmother told me: "That's what I heard in the sermon." And my father smiled. And he ate with a good appetite and even let his food digest leisurely beside the railing, silent, his eyes closed, but not sleeping, as if to think that he was dreaming while awake.

It rained all afternoon in a single tone. In the uniform and peaceful intensity you could hear the water fall, the way it is when you travel all afternoon on a train. But without our noticing it, the rain was penetrating too deeply into our senses. Early Monday morning, when we closed the door to avoid the cutting, icy draft that blew in from the courtyard, our senses had been filled with rain. And on Monday morning they had overflowed. My stepmother and I went back to look at the garden. The harsh gray earth of May had been changed overnight into a dark, sticky substance like cheap soap. A trickle of water began to run off the flowerpots. "I think they had more than enough water during the night," my stepmother said. And I noticed that she had stopped smiling and that her joy of the previous day had changed during the night into a lax and tedious seriousness. "I think you're right," I said. "It would be better to have the Indians put them on the veranda until it stops raining." And that was what they did, while the rain grew like an immense tree over the other trees. My father occupied the same spot where he had been on Sunday afternoon, but he didn't talk about the rain. He said: "I must have slept poorly last night because I woke up with a stiff back." And he stayed there, sitting by the railing with his feet on a chair and his head turned toward the empty garden. Only at dusk, after he had turned down lunch, did he say: "It looks as if it will never clear." And I remembered the months of heat. I remembered August, those long and awesome siestas in which we dropped down to die under the weight of the hour, our clothes sticking to our bodies, hearing outside the insistent and dull buzzing of the hour that never passed. I saw the washed-down walls, the joints of the beams all puffed up by the water. I saw the small garden, empty for the first time, and the jasmine bush against the wall, faithful to the memory of my mother. I saw my father sitting in a rocker, his painful vertebrae resting on a pillow and his sad eyes lost in the labyrinth of the rain. I remembered the August nights in whose wondrous silence nothing could be heard except the millenary sound that the earth makes as it spins on its rusty, unoiled axis. Suddenly I felt overcome by an overwhelming sadness.

It rained all Monday, just like Sunday. But now it seemed to be raining in another way, because something different and bitter was going on in my heart. At dusk a voice beside my chair said: "This rain is a bore." Without turning to look, I recognized Martín's voice. I knew that he was speaking in the next chair, with the same cold and awesome expression that hadn't varied, not even after that gloomy December dawn when he started being my husband. Five months had passed since then. Now I was going to have a child. And Martín was there beside me saying that the rain bored him. "Not a bore," I said. "It seems terribly sad to me, with the empty garden and those poor trees that can't come in from the courtyard." Then I turned to look at him and Martín was no longer there. It was only a voice that was saying to me: "It doesn't look as if it will ever clear," and when I looked toward the voice I found only the empty chair.

On Tuesday morning we found a cow in the garden. It looked like a clay promontory in its hard and rebellious immobility, its hooves sunken in the mud and its head bent over. During the morning the Indians tried to drive it away with sticks and stones. But the cow stayed there, imperturbable in the garden, hard, inviolable, its hooves still sunken in the mud and its huge head humiliated by the rain. The Indians harassed it until my father's patient tolerance came to its defense. "Leave her alone," he said. "She'll leave the way she came."

At sundown on Tuesday the water tightened and hurt, like a shroud over the heart. The coolness of the first morning began to change into a hot and sticky humidity. The temperature was neither cold nor hot; it was the temperature of a fever chill. Feet sweated inside shoes. It was hard to say what was more disagreeable, bare skin or the contact of clothing on skin. All activity had ceased in the house. We sat on the veranda but we no longer watched the rain as we did on the first day. We no longer felt it falling. We no longer saw anything except the outline of the trees in the mist, with a sad and desolate sunset which left on your lips the same taste with which you awaken after having dreamed about a stranger. I knew that it was Tuesday and I remembered the twins of Saint Jerome, the blind girls who came to the house every week to sing us simple songs, saddened by the bitter and unprotected prodigy of their voices. Above the rain I heard the blind twins' little song and I imagined them at home, huddling, waiting for the rain to stop so they could go out and sing. The twins of Saint Jerome wouldn't come that day, I-thought, nor would the beggar woman be on the veranda after siesta, asking, as on every Tuesday, for the eternal branch of lemon balm.

That day we lost track of meals. At siesta time my stepmother served a plate of tasteless soup and a piece of stale bread. But actually we hadn't eaten since sunset on Monday and I think that from then on we stopped thinking. We were paralyzed, drugged by the rain, given over to the collapse of nature with a peaceful and resigned attitude. Only the cow was moving in the afternoon. Suddenly a deep noise shook her insides and her hooves sank into the mud with greater force. Then she stood motionless for half an hour, as if she were already dead but could not fall down because the habit of being alive prevented her, the habit of remaining in one position in the rain, until the habit grew weaker than her body. Then she doubled her front legs (her dark and shiny haunches still raised in a last agonized effort) and sank her drooling snout into the mud, finally surrendering to the weight of her own matter in a silent, gradual, and dignified ceremony of total downfall. "She got that far," someone said behind me. And

I turned to look and on the threshold I saw the Tuesday beggar woman who had come through the storm to ask for the branch of lemon balm.

Perhaps on Wednesday I might have grown accustomed to that overwhelming atmosphere if on going to the living room I hadn't found the table pushed against the wall, the furniture piled on top of it, and on the other side, on a parapet prepared during the night, trunks and boxes of household utensils. The spectacle produced a terrible feeling of emptiness in me. Something had happened during the night. The house was in disarray; the Guajiro Indians, shirtless and barefoot, with their pants rolled up to their knees, were carrying the furniture into the dining room. In the men's expression, in the very diligence with which they were working, one could see the cruelty of their frustrated rebellion, of their necessary and humiliating inferiority in the rain. I moved without direction, without will. I felt changed into a desolate meadow sown with algae and lichens, with soft, sticky toadstools, fertilized by the repugnant plants of dampness and shadows. I was in the living room contemplating the desert spectacle of the piled-up furniture when I heard my stepmother's voice warning me from her room that I might catch pneumonia. Only then did I realize that the water was up to my ankles, that the house was flooded, the floor covered by a thick surface of viscous, dead water.

On Wednesday noon it still hadn't finished dawning. And before three o'clock in the afternoon night had come on completely, ahead of time and sickly, with the same slow, monotonous, and pitiless rhythm of the rain in the courtyard. It was a premature dusk, soft and lugubrious, growing in the midst of the silence of the Guajiros, who were squatting on the chairs against the walls, defeated and impotent against the disturbance of nature. That was when news began to arrive from outside. No one brought it to the house. It simply arrived, precise, individualized, as if led by the liquid clay that ran through the streets and dragged household items along, things and more things, the leftovers of a remote catastrophe, rubbish and dead animals. Events that took place on Sunday, when the rain was still the announcement of a providential season, took two days to be known at our house. And on Wednesday the news arrived as if impelled by the very inner dynamism of the storm. It was learned then that the church was flooded and its collapse expected. Someone who had no reason to know said that night: "The train hasn't been able to cross the bridge since Monday. It seems that the river carried away the tracks." And it was learned that a sick woman had disappeared from her bed and had been found that afternoon floating in the courtyard.

Terrified, possessed by the fright and the deluge, I sat down in the rocker with my legs tucked up and my eyes fixed on the damp darkness full of hazy foreboding. My stepmother appeared in the doorway with the lamp held high and her head erect. She looked like a family ghost before whom I felt no fear whatever because I myself shared her supernatural condition. She came over to where I was. She still held her head high and the lamp in the air, and she splashed through the water on the veranda. "Now we have to pray," she said. And I noticed her dry and wrinkled face, as if she had just left her tomb or as if she had been made of some substance different from human matter. She was across from me with her rosary in her hand saying: "Now we have to pray. The water broke open the tombs and now the poor dead are floating in the cemetery."

I may have slept a little that night when I awoke with a start because of a sour and penetrating smell like that of decomposing bodies. I gave a strong shake to Martín, who was snoring beside me. "Don't you notice it?" I asked him. And he said: "What?" And I said: "The smell. It must be the dead people floating along the streets." I was terrified by that idea, but Martín turned to the wall and with a husky and sleepy voice said: "That's something you made up. Pregnant women are always imagining things."

At dawn on Thursday the smells stopped, the sense of distance was lost. The notion of time, upset since the day before, disappeared completely. Then there was no Thursday. What should have been Thursday was a physical, jellylike thing that could have been parted with the hands in order to look into Friday. There were no men or women there. My stepmother, my father, the Indians were adipose and improbable bodies that moved in the marsh of winter. My father said to me: "Don't move away from here until you're told what to do," and his voice was distant and indirect and didn't seem to be perceived by the ear but by touch, which was the only sense that remained active.

But my father didn't return: he got lost in the weather. So when night came I called my stepmother to tell her to accompany me to my bedroom. I had a peaceful and serene sleep, which lasted all through the night. On the following day the atmosphere was still the same, colorless, odorless, and without any temperature. As soon as I awoke I jumped into a chair and remained there without moving, because something told me that there was still a region of my consciousness that hadn't awakened completely. Then I heard the train whistle. The prolonged and sad whistle of the train fleeing the storm. *It must have cleared somewhere,* I thought, and a voice behind me seemed to answer my thought. "Where?" it said. "Who's there?" I asked looking. And I saw my stepmother with a long thin arm in the direction of the wall. "It's me," she said. And I asked her: "Can you hear it?" And she said yes, maybe it had cleared on the outskirts and they'd repaired the tracks. Then she gave me a tray with some steaming breakfast. It smelled of garlic sauce and boiled butter. It was a plate of soup. Disconcerted, I asked my stepmother what time it was. And she, calmly, with a voice that tasted of prostrated resignation, said: "It must be around two-thirty. The train isn't late after all this." I said: "Two-thirty! How could I have slept so long!" And she said: "You haven't slept very long. It can't be more than three o'clock." And I, trembling, feeling the plate slip through my fingers: "Two-thirty on Friday," I said. And she, monstrously tranquil: "Two-thirty on Thursday, child. *Still* two-thirty on Thursday."

I don't know how long I was sunken in that somnambulism where the senses lose their value. I only know that after many uncountable hours I heard a voice in the next room. A voice that said: "Now you can roll the bed to this side." It was a tired voice, but not the voice of a sick person, rather that of a convalescent. Then I heard the sound of the bricks in the water. I remained rigid before I realized that I was in a horizontal position. Then I felt the immense emptiness. I felt the wavering and violent silence of the house, the incredible immobility that affected everything. And suddenly I felt my heart turned into a frozen stone. *I'm dead,* I thought. *My God, I'm dead.* I gave a jump in the bed. I shouted: "Ada! Ada!" Martín's unpleasant voice answered me from the other side. "They can't hear you, they're already outside by now." Only then did I realize that it had cleared and that all around us a silence stretched out, a tranquillity, a mysterious and deep beatitude, a perfect state which must have been very much like death. Then footsteps could be heard on the veranda. A clear and completely living voice was heard. Then a cool breeze shook the panel of the door, made the doorknob squeak, and a solid and monumental body, like a ripe fruit, fell deeply into the cistern in the courtyard. Something in the air revealed the presence of an invisible person who was smiling in the darkness. *Good Lord,* I thought then, confused by the mixup in time. *It wouldn't surprise me now if they were coming to call me to go to last Sunday's mass.*

(1955)

Nabo

THE BLACK MAN WHO MADE
THE ANGELS WAIT . . .

Nabo was lying face down in the hay. He felt the smell of a
urinated stable rubbing on his body. On his brown and shiny skin
he felt the warm embers of the last horses, but he couldn't feel
the skin. Nabo couldn't feel anything. It was as if he'd gone to
sleep with the last blow of the horseshoe on his forehead and
now that was the only feeling he had. He opened his eyes. He
closed them again and then was quiet, stretched out, stiff, as he
had been all afternoon, feeling himself growing without time, until
someone behind him said: "Come on, Nabo. You've slept enough
already." He turned over and didn't see the horses; the door was
closed. Nabo must have imagined that the animals were somewhere in the darkness in spite of the fact that he couldn't hear
their impatient stamping. He imagined that the person speaking
to him was doing it from outside the stable, because the door
was closed from the inside and barred. Once more the voice behind him said: "That's right, Nabo, you've slept enough already.
You've been asleep for almost three days." Only then did Nabo
open his eyes completely and remember: "I'm here because a horse
kicked me."

He didn't know what hour he was living. The days had been
left behind. It was as if someone had passed a damp sponge over

those remote Saturday nights when he used to go to the town square. He forgot about the white shirt. He forgot that he had a green hat made of green straw and dark pants. He forgot that he didn't have any shoes. Nabo would go to the square on Saturday nights and sit in a corner, silent, not to listen to the music but to watch the black man. Every Saturday he saw him. The Negro wore horn-rimmed glasses, tied to his ears, and he played the saxophone at one of the rear music stands. Nabo saw the black man but the black man didn't see Nabo. At least, if someone had known that Nabo went to the square on Saturday nights to see the Negro and had asked him (not now, because he couldn't remember) whether the black man had ever seen him, Nabo would have said no. It was the only thing he did after currying the horses: watch the black man.

One Saturday the Negro wasn't at his place in the band. Nabo probably thought at first that he wasn't going to play anymore in the public concerts in spite of the fact that the music stand was there. Although for that reason precisely, the fact that the music stand was there, he thought later that the Negro would be back the following Saturday. But on the following Saturday he wasn't back and the music stand wasn't in its place.

Nabo rolled onto one side and he saw the man talking to him. At first he didn't recognize him, blotted out by the darkness of the stable. The man was sitting on a jutting beam, talking and patting his knees. "A horse kicked me," Nabo said again, trying to recognize the man. "That's right," the man said. "The horses aren't here now and we're waiting for you in the choir." Nabo shook his head. He still hadn't begun to think, but now he thought he'd seen the man somewhere. Nabo didn't understand, but he didn't find it strange either that someone should say that to him, because every day while he curried the horses he invented songs to distract them. Then he would sing the same songs he sang to the horses in the living room to distract the mute girl. When he was singing if someone had told him that he was taking him to a choir, it wouldn't have surprised him. Now he was surprised even less because he didn't understand. He was fatigued, dulled, brutish. "I want to know where the horses are," he said. And the man said: "I already told you, the horses aren't here. All we're interested in is to get a voice like yours." And perhaps, face down in the hay, Nabo heard, but he couldn't distinguish the pain that the horseshoe had left on his forehead from his other disordered sensations. He turned his head on the hay and fell asleep.

Nabo still went to the square for two or three weeks in spite of the fact that the Negro was no longer in the band. Perhaps someone would have answered him if Nabo had asked what had happened to the black man. But he didn't ask and kept on going to the concerts until another man with another saxophone came to take the Negro's spot. Then Nabo was convinced that the Negro wouldn't be back and he decided not to return to the square. When he awoke he thought he had slept a very short time. The smell of damp hay still burned in his nose. The darkness was still there before his eyes, surrounding him. And the man was still in the corner. The obscure and peaceful voice of the man who patted his knees, saying: "We're waiting for you, Nabo. You've been asleep for almost two years and you refuse to get up." Then Nabo closed his eyes again. He opened them again, kept looking at the corner, and saw the man once more, disoriented, perplexed. Only then did he recognize him.

If the people in the house had known what Nabo was doing on the square on Saturday nights, they probably would have thought that when he stopped going he did so because now he had music at home. That was when we brought the gramophone to amuse the girl. Since it needed someone to wind it up all day, it seemed most natural that that person should be Nabo. He could do it when he didn't have to take care of the horses. The girl remained seated, listening to the records. Sometimes, when the music was playing, the girl would get out of her chair, still looking at the wall, drooling, and would drag herself to the veranda. Nabo would lift the needle and start to sing. In the beginning, when he first came to the house and we asked him what he could do, Nabo said that he could sing. But that didn't interest anyone. What we needed was a boy to curry the horses. Nabo stayed, but he kept on singing, as if we had hired him to sing and the business of currying the horses was only a distraction that made the work easier. That went on for more than a year, until those of us in the house grew used to the idea that the girl would never be able to walk, would never recognize anyone, would always be the little dead and lonely girl who listened to the gramophone looking coldly at the wall until we lifted her out of her chair and took her to her room. Then she ceased to pain us, but Nabo was still faithful, punctual, cranking the gramophone. That was during the time when Nabo was still going to the square on Saturday nights. One day, when the boy was in the stable, someone beside the gramophone said: "Nabo!" We were on the veranda, not concerned about something no one could have said. But when we heard it a second time: "Nabo!" we raised our heads and asked: "Who's with the girl?" And someone said: "I didn't see anyone come in." And another said: "I'm sure I heard a voice calling Nabo." But when we went to look all we found was the girl on the floor, leaning against the wall.

Nabo came back early and went to bed. It was the following Saturday that he didn't return to the square because the Negro had been replaced. And three weeks later, on a Monday, the gramophone began to play while Nabo was in the stable. No one worried at first. Only later, when we saw the black boy coming, singing and still dripping from the water of the horses, did we ask him: "How'd you get out?" He said: "Through the door. I've been in the stable since noon." "The gramophone's playing. Can't you hear it?" we asked him. And Nabo said he could. And we asked him: "Who wound it up?" And he, shrugging his shoulders: "The girl. She's been winding it for a long time now."

That was the way things were until the day we found him lying face down on the hay, locked in the stable and with the edge of the horseshoe encrusted on his forehead. When we picked him up by the shoulders, Nabo said: "I'm here because a horse kicked me." But no one was interested in what he might have said. We were interested in his cold, dead eyes and mouth full of green froth. He spent the whole night weeping, burning with fever, delirious, talking about the comb that he'd lost in the hay in the stable. That was the first day. On the following day, when he opened his eyes and said: "I'm thirsty," and we brought him water, he drank it all down in one swallow and twice asked for a little more. We asked him how he felt and he said: "I feel as if a horse had kicked me." And he kept on talking all day and all night. And finally he sat up in bed, pointed up with his fore-finger, and said that the galloping of the horses had kept him awake all night. But he'd had no fever since the night before. He was no longer delirious, but he kept on talking until they put a handkerchief in his mouth. Then Nabo began to sing behind the handkerchief, saying that next to his ear he could hear the breathing of the blind horses looking for water on top of the closed door. When we took out the handkerchief so that he could eat something, he turned toward the wall and we all thought that he'd fallen asleep and it was even possible that he had fallen asleep for a while. But when he awoke he was no longer on the bed. His feet were tied and his hands were tied to a brace beam in the room. Trussed up, Nabo began to sing.

When he recognized him, Nabo said to the man: "I've seen you before." And the man said: "Every Saturday you used to watch me in the square." And Nabo said: "That's right, but I thought I saw you and you didn't see me." And the man said: "I never saw you, but later on, when I stopped coming, I felt as if someone had stopped watching me on Saturdays." And Nabo said: "You never came back, but I kept on going for three or four weeks." And the man, still not moving, patting himself on the knees: "I couldn't go back to the square even though it was the only thing that was worth anything." Nabo tried to sit up, shook his head in the hay, and still he heard the cold, obstinate voice, until he no longer had time even to know that he was falling asleep again. Always, ever since the horse had kicked him, that happened. And he always heard the voice: "We're waiting for you, Nabo. There's no longer any way to measure the time you've been asleep."

Four weeks after the Negro had stopped coming to the band, Nabo was combing the tail of one of the horses. He'd never done that. He would just curry them and sing in the meantime. But on Wednesday he'd gone to the market and had seen a comb and had said to himself: "That comb is for combing the horses' tails." That was when the whole thing happened with the horse that gave him a kick and left him all mixed up for the rest of his life, ten or fifteen years before. Somebody in the house said: "It would have been better if he'd died that day and hadn't gone on like this, all through, talking nonsense for the rest of his life." But no one had seen him again ever since the day we locked him up. Only we knew that he was there, locked up in the room, and since then the girl hadn't moved the gramophone again. But in the house we had very little interest in knowing about it. We'd locked him up as if he were a horse, as if the kick had passed the sluggishness on to him and encrusted on his forehead was all the stupidity of horses: animalness. And we left him isolated within four walls as if we'd decided he should die of imprisonment because we weren't cold-blooded enough to kill him in any other way. Fourteen years passed like that until one of the children grew up and said he had the urge to see his face. And he opened the door.

Nabo saw the man again. "A horse kicked me," he said. And the man said: "You've been saying that for centuries and in the meantime we've been waiting for you in the choir." Nabo shook his head again, sank his wounded forehead into the hay once more, and thought he suddenly remembered how things had happened. "It was the first time I ever combed a horse's tail," he said. And the man said: "We wanted it that way so you would come and sing in the choir." And Nabo said: "I shouldn't have bought the comb." And the man said: "You would have come across it in any case. We'd decided that you'd find the comb and comb the horses' tails." And Nabo said: "I'd never stood behind them before." And the man, still tranquil, still not showing impatience: "But you did stand there and the horse kicked you. It was the only way for you to come to the c'.oir." And the conversation, implacable, daily, went on until someone in the house said: "It must be fifteen years since anyone opened that door." The girl (she hadn't grown, she was over thirty and was beginning to get sad in her eyelids) was sitting looking at the wall when they opened the door. She turned her face in the other direction, sniffing. And when they closed the door, they said again: "Nabo's peaceful. There's nothing moving inside anymore. One of these days he'll die and we won't be able to tell except for the smell." And someone said: "We can tell by the food. He's never stopped eating. He's fine like that, locked up with no one to bother him. He gets good light from the rear side." And things stayed like that; except that the girl kept on looking toward the door, sniffing the warm fumes that filtered through the cracks. She stayed like that until early in the morning, when we heard a metallic sound in the living room and we remembered that it was the same sound that had been heard fifteen years before when Nabo was winding the gramophone. We got up, lighted the lamp, and heard the first measures of the forgotten song; the sad song that had been dead on the records for such a long time. The sound kept on, more and more strained, until a dry sound was heard at the instant we reached the living room, and we could still hear the record playing and saw the girl in the corner beside the gramophone, looking at the wall and holding up the crank. We didn't say anything, but went back to our rooms remembering that someone had told us sometime that the girl knew how to crank the gramophone. Thinking that, we stayed awake, listening to the worn little tune from the record that was still spinning on what was left of the broken spring.

The day before, when they opened the door, it smelled of biological waste, of a dead body. The one who had opened it shouted: "Nabo! Nabo!" But nobody answered from inside. Beside the opening was the empty plate. Three times a day the plate was put under the door and three times a day the plate came out again with no food on it. That was how we knew that Nabo was alive. But by no other means. There was no more moving inside, no more singing. And it must have been after they closed the door that Nabo said to the man: "I can't go to the choir." And the man asked why. And Nabo said: "Because I haven't got any shoes." And the man, raising his feet, said: "That doesn't matter. Nobody wear shoes here." And Nabo saw the hard, yellow soles of the bare feet the man was holding up. "I've been waiting for you here for an eternity," the man said. "The horse only kicked me a moment ago," Nabo said. "Now I'll throw a little water on my face and take them out for a walk." And the man said: "The horses don't need you anymore. There aren't any more horses. You're the one who should come with us." And Nabo said: "The horses should have been here." He got up a little, sank his hands into the hay while the man said: "They haven't had anyone to look after them for fifteen years." But Nabo was scratching the ground under the hay, saying: "The comb must still be here." And the man said: "They closed up the stable fifteen years ago. It's full of rubbish now." And Nabo said: "Rubbish doesn't collect in one afternoon. Until I find the comb I won't move out of here."

On the following day, after they'd fastened the door again, they heard the difficult movements inside once more. No one moved afterward. No one said anything again when the first creaks were heard and the door began to give way under unusual pressure. Inside something like the panting of a penned animal was heard. Finally the groan of rusty hinges was heard as they broke when Nabo shook his head again. "Until I find the comb, I won't go to the choir," he said. "It must be around here somewhere." And he dug in the hay, breaking it, scratching the ground, until the man said: "All right Nabo. If the only thing you're waiting for to come to the choir is to find the comb, go look for it." He leaned forward, his face darkened by a patient haughtiness. He put his hands against the barrier and said: "Go ahead, Nabo. I'll see that nobody stops you."

And then the door gave way and the huge bestial Negro with the harsh scar marked on his forehead (in spite of the fact that fifteen years had passed) came out stumbling over the furniture, his fists raised and menacing, still with the rope they had tied him with fifteen years before (when he was a little black boy who looked after the horses); and (before reaching the courtyard) he passed by the girl, who remained seated, the crank of the gramophone still in her hand since the night before (when she saw the unchained black force she remembered something that at one time must have been a word) and he reached the courtyard (before finding the stable), after having knocked down the living-room mirror with his shoulder, but without seeing the girl (neither beside the gramophone nor in the mirror), and he stood with his face to the sun, his eyes closed, blind (while inside the noise of the broken mirror was still going on), and he ran aimlessly, like a blindfolded horse instinctively looking for the stable door that fifteen years of imprisonment had erased from his memory but not from his instincts (since that remote day when he had combed the horse's tail and was left befuddled for the rest of his life), and leaving behind catastrophe, dissolution, and chaos like a blindfolded bull in a roomful of lamps, he reached the back yard (still without finding the stable), and scratched on the ground with the tempestuous fury with which he had knocked down the mirror, thinking perhaps that by scratching on the ground he could make the smell of mare's urine rise up again, until he finally reached the stable doors and pushed them too soon, falling inside on his face, in his death agony perhaps, but still confused by that fierce animalness that a half-second before had prevented him from hearing the girl, who raised the crank when she heard him pass and remembered, drooling, but without moving from the chair, without moving her mouth but twirling the crank of the gramophone in the air, remembered the only word she had ever learned to say in her life, and she shouted it from the living room: "Nabo! Nabo!"

(1951)

Gabriel García Márquez
In Evil Hour £5.99

The people of the nameless small town in the nameless South American republic face, as usual, a dripping, sweaty autumn. The rain falls in torrents, the mice are eating the church foundations, the people groan under a far-away dictatorship. Someone starts nailing lampoons to people's doorways at night. There is a shooting. The mayor (and chief of police) dawdles cynically into action, which can only mean more tragedy . . .

'Not just about one specific bad time but about all times when doubt, secrets, corruption, double-dealing and guilt come to a head . . . a masterly book' GUARDIAN

'An obvious masterpiece' AUBERON WAUGH

One Hundred Years of Solitude £6.99

A band of adventurers establish a town in the heart of the South American jungle. The occasion marks the beginning: of the world, of a great family, of a century of extraordinary events, and of an extraordinary novel.

'Sweeping, chaotic brilliance, often more poetry than prose . . . one vast and musical saga' THE TIMES

'A classic on the grandest scale . . . Márquez is a spellbinder' SPECTATOR

Chronicle of a Death Foretold £4.99

'Marquez uses the device of an unnamed, shadowy narrator visiting the scene of the killing many years later . . . The book and its narrator probe slowly, painfully, through the mists of half-accurate memories . . . and achieve only provisional answers' SALMAN RUSHDIE, LONDON REVIEW OF BOOKS

'As a fable of that madness which only obscure principles can produce, *Chronicle* is hypnotic. But what fascinates further is the leisurely, almost desultory artistry with which Márquez extends an incident into an event' NEW STATESMAN

'In the hands of a master the telling of a simple tale can be pure art' DAILY TELEGRAPH

'Clearly establishes Márquez as one of the most accomplished and the most magical of political novelists writing today' THE TIMES LITERARY SUPPLEMENT

Italo Calvino
If on a Winter's Night a Traveller £4.99

A fiction about fictions, a novel about novels, a book about books. Its chief protagonists are its author and his reader. Its progress traces the reading of a novel and the consummation of a love affair. In its course a whole shelf of novels are begun and – for reasons at the time entirely reasonable – never finished. Its characters are the myriads of beings involved with the process of creation, construction and consumption of The Book.

'I can think of no finer writer to have beside me while Italy explodes, while Britain burns, while the world ends'
SALMAN RUSHDIE, LONDON REVIEW OF BOOKS

Invisible Cities £4.99

'This most beautiful of all his books throws up ideas, allusions, and breathtaking imaginative insights on almost every page. Each time he returns from his travels, Marco Polo is invited by Kublai Khan to describe the cities he has visited. The conqueror and explorer exchange visions: for Kublai Khan the world is constantly expanding; for Marco Polo, who has seen so much of it, it is an ever-diminishing place . . . Calvino is describing only one city in his book. Venice, that decaying heap of incomparable splendour, still stands as substantial evidence of man's ability to create something perfect out of chaos . . .' TIMES LITERARY SUPPLEMENT

'The cities correspond to psychological states and historical states, possibilities and transformations' LISTENER

All Pan books are available at your local bookshop or newsagent, or can be ordered direct from the publisher. Indicate the number of copies required and fill in the form below.

Send to: Pan C. S. Dept
             Macmillan Distribution Ltd
             Houndmills Basingstoke RG21 2XS
or phone: 0256 29242, quoting title, author and Credit Card number.

Please enclose a remittance* to the value of the cover price plus: £1.00 for the first book plus 50p per copy for each additional book ordered.

*Payment may be made in sterling by UK personal cheque, postal order, sterling draft or international money order, made payable to Pan Books Ltd.

Alternatively by Barclaycard/Access/Amex/Diners

Card No.

Expiry Date

Signature:

Applicable only in the UK and BFPO addresses

While every effort is made to keep prices low, it is sometimes necessary to increase prices at short notice. Pan Books reserve the right to show on covers and charge new retail prices which may differ from those advertised in the text or elsewhere.

NAME AND ADDRESS IN BLOCK LETTERS PLEASE:

....

Name _____

Address_____

_____

_____

_____

6/92